Pictures of Me

PICTURES of ME

By Marilee Haynes

Pauline
BOOKS & MEDIA
Boston

Library of Congress Cataloging-in-Publication Data

Haynes, Marilee, author.
  Pictures of me / by Marilee Haynes.
      pages cm
  Summary: This year the "fifth-farewell" project at St. Joe is to make a meaningful picture of yourself and present it to the rest of the class, and Annie, who has a horror of public speaking, is terrified, especially since most of the other children make fun of her; but Annie collects words, and when a boy she likes suggests that she use her collection, it gives her an idea--if she can find the courage to present it.

  ISBN 978-0-8198-6019-4 (pbk.) -- ISBN 0-8198-6019-0 (pbk.) 1. Stage fright--Juvenile fiction. 2. Identity (Psychology)--Juvenile fiction. 3. Self-confidence--Juvenile fiction. 4. Bullying--Juvenile fiction. 5. Friendship--Juvenile fiction. 6. Families--Michigan--Juvenile fiction. 7. Catholic schools--Juvenile fiction. [1. Stage fright--Fiction. 2. Identity--Fiction. 3. Self-confidence--Fiction. 4. Bullying--Fiction. 5. Friendship--Fiction. 6. Family life--Michigan--Fiction. 7. Catholic schools--Fiction. 8. Schools--Fiction. 9. Michigan--Fiction.] I. Title.
  PZ7.H3149146Pi 2016
  813.6--dc23
  [Fic]

                                      2015020772

Book design by Mary Joseph Peterson, FSP

Cover and interior illustrations by Jennifer Kalis

Published by Pauline Books & Media, 50 Saint Paul's Avenue, Boston, MA 02130–3491

Printed in the U.S.A.

POM VSAUSAPEOILL9-110052 6019-0

www.pauline.org

Pauline Books & Media is the publishing house of the Daughters of St. Paul, an international congregation of women religious serving the Church with the communications media.

1 2 3 4 5 6 7 8 9   20 19 18 17 16

*This book is about courage and friendship.
It's also about the love
between mothers and daughters.
I dedicate it to my mom
and to my two precious daughters.*

word #983

conundrum

a puzzling question or problem

M r. Summer tears off another number on the countdown chart. Only forty-eight days left until the end of fifth grade. And today's the day we finally find out about our project—The Fifth Farewell. It's a St. Joe's tradition as old as our school, which is as old as our town, which makes it a big deal. I can't explain what's so important about it. It just is. It always has been. I guess it's like saying goodbye to elementary school.

I squirm around in the most uncomfortable chair in the universe, trying to find a comfortable spot. Nothing works. Sitting up perfectly straight with my shoulders back and both feet flat on the floor—the kind of posture that makes my mom smile? Nope. Tucking one leg under me and wrapping the other one around my chair leg? Still, no. Oh, well. I rest my chin on my hand. And wait.

There it is.

From down the hall comes the sound of sneakers slapping against the floor. The slapping gets louder as the sneaker-wearer gets closer. Then three beats of silence before a locker door slams. And right on cue, my best friend, Taylor Matthews —her black, curly hair flying in all directions— bounds into the classroom.

"Hey, Annie." Taylor skids past my desk at the exact moment the bell rings, just like she does every day.

"You made it." I grin.

Taylor smiles back at me with all of her teeth— and all of her braces—and flops into her chair.

"Okay, class. Let's get started," says Mr. Summer. I think it's funny that our teacher's name is Mr. Summer since summer is the only time kids don't have to think about teachers. But it's not summer vacation yet—not for forty-eight more days. I slide my notebook and sparkly pen out of my desk.

"It's time to reveal some of the specifics of this year's Fifth Farewell." Mr. Summer writes the name of the project on the smart board in giant letters. I write the same thing at the top of a blank page in my notebook in much smaller letters.

"I want this project to inspire you and hopefully get your creative juices flowing," he says. Snorting laughs and gagging sounds from around the room mean the boys think there's something disgusting and funny about the thought of someone's flowing juices. They have a point.

Mr. Summer slides his glasses back up his nose and waits for quiet. "We're doing something a little different this year." Different how? Different why? The Fifth Farewell is usually an essay or a poem. Last year's fifth grade interviewed all the teachers in the school and made a class newspaper. Those are good ideas. Regular ideas. Also, since words and writing are two of my very favorite things, they are things I'm good at.

"For *your* Fifth Farewell, I want each of you to create a self-portrait and present it to the class." My pen slips out of my hand and falls to the floor. I leave it there. Mr. Summer keeps talking. "Your self-portrait should tell us who you are and, if you choose, who you want to be. That's all I'm going to give you in the way of instructions for now." He looks around the room and beams at us. I don't beam back because any idea that includes the words "present it to the class" isn't something to smile about. Not. One. Bit.

The speaker next to the clock crackles and the voice of our principal, Father Richard, comes on.

Chairs slide back as we all rise, and stand next to our desks—almost like a dance. Prayers come first, followed by the Pledge of Allegiance, and then announcements. It's the same as every day. My lips move automatically, praying and pledging along with the rest of my class.

In the middle of Father Richard's description of today's disgusting-sounding hot lunch menu, Jalen Moore pokes me in the back with his finger. Sitting in front of Jalen means getting poked just like that—in the same spot—at least fifteen times a day. "What are you going to do?"

I shrug without turning around, or picking up my pen, or breathing much.

Out of all the words Mr. Summer said about our project, five of them bounce around inside my brain over and over again. I scribble a word that sums it all up on a scrap of paper and tuck it into my pocket. *Conundrum*. It doesn't matter if I know what a Mr. Summer-version of a self-portrait is supposed to look like. I mostly don't. But even if I did and even if I made something completely amazing, there's one thing I can't do. One thing I won't do.

Present it to the class.

When the bell finally rings for lunch, I bend over to pick up my backpack and two identical pairs of shoes come into view. I look up to see two nearly identical girls with identical, snotty looks on their faces: Madison Marinelli and Addison Kim. Fabulous.

"Hey, Puddles," says one of the girls. It doesn't actually matter which one. "What are you going to do for your presentation? Or will you chicken out again, like always?" Madison makes what I guess is supposed to be a clucking sound and they both walk away, laughing and clutching each other's arms.

These are the popular girls in the fifth grade. Why they are popular is a mystery. They aren't nice to anyone and have no other friends. Still, they have power. They like making the rest of us miserable. And they're good at it.

Madison and Addison started calling me Puddles halfway through second grade. Well, Madison started it and, like always, Addison just followed along.

There's a reason they call me Puddles—a horrible, humiliating, wake-up-in-the-middle-of-the-night-thinking-that-it-happened-all-over-again reason. And that's why I have a *conundrum*. If our Fifth Farewell means getting up in front of the class and presenting something, I'm going to fail because I won't do it.

I can't.

word #984

inkling

a partial idea or understanding

The rest of the day goes by without any other unpleasant surprises or insults. Sometimes that's the best you can get from a day in fifth grade. We were reminded that we have a science test tomorrow. Ugh. I'm terrible at science. This does not make my dad happy. He's an actual scientist with microscopes and a white lab coat and beakers. He hopes I'll be one, too. Fat chance. And not just because the enormous safety goggles hurt my nose. Luckily, Taylor is a genius at science and she always helps me study.

This morning while I was scarfing down my bowl of cereal, Mom told me Taylor is coming home from school with me today, but not for a fun reason. Taylor's parents are taking her little brother Zach to see another new doctor.

Zach is four years old and super cute. He has the same curly, black hair and brown eyes as Taylor, but not her smile. He almost never smiles. Zach has a hard time talking to people and playing with other kids. Mr. and Mrs. Matthews took him to a lot of doctors before they found out what was wrong. Taylor says she doesn't want to talk about it. So we don't. And she doesn't want anyone else to know. So no one else does.

When school is over for the day, Taylor and I come in the front door, kick off our shoes and drop our backpacks.

"Come on." I start walking toward the kitchen.

"Wait." Taylor holds herself perfectly still, closes her eyes and breaths in through her nose—loudly.

"Cheese." Another sniff. "Tomato sauce." A third sniff, the biggest one yet. "Pineapple." Taylor's eyes open and she starts race-walking toward the kitchen, dragging me along behind her.

"Hi, girls," says my mom. "The pizza just came out of the oven. Be careful, it's still hot." Mom passes us each a plate with a giant slice on it. Almost before she finishes talking, Taylor and I each take a gigantic bite. Yum! Totally worth burning the roof of my mouth.

"Did you have a good day?"

Before I answer, I take another bite of pizza, even bigger this time. I take my time chewing thoroughly and wash it down with two big gulps of water.

"Well, Mr. Summer told us what we have to do for our Fifth Farewell," I say.

"Yeah, Mrs. Humphrey. Annie's been freaking out about it all day." I dig my elbow into Taylor's side which she totally knows means "shut up, right now." It doesn't work. Probably because my mom plops another piece of pizza onto Taylor's plate—one with extra pineapple. She knows—and I know—Taylor is powerless against pizza, especially pineapple pizza. It makes her talk more.

"So we're supposed to do some kind of self-portrait, right? It was kind of confusing, but I figure I'll just do a collage with some pictures of me and a bunch of stuff I like. You know, pizza, cupcakes, cookies, oh and other stuff besides food." Taylor giggles. "I must be hungry."

"Annie, you can do a scrapbook," says my mom. "We have plenty of pictures. And I can help you. It'll be fun!" She claps her hands . . . twice.

Oh, no. My mom is crazy for scrapbooks. My little sister Daisy and I star in enough scrapbooks to fill an entire bookshelf in our family room. Nothing's too boring to earn a page of honor in one of my mom's scrapbooks.

I am not a scrapbooker.

"Thanks for the idea, Mom. Not sure about a scrapbook. I'll think of something." I try not to roll my eyes. I don't want to hurt her feelings, but I need to put a stop to this scrapbook idea before she gets out the fancy paper and special scissors.

"And we have to present our projects," I say it kind of casual and drink the rest of my water.

"Oh?" My mom brushes some crumbs off the counter, not looking at me. "Present them to whom?"

"Our class, I guess," I say. "But Mr. Summer didn't really say. Do you think we'll have to do it in front of all the parents, too? Or the whole school?" My voice goes higher and higher. It's possible I'm forgetting to breathe. I grip Taylor's arm a bit too hard. She squeaks.

My mom looks at me with her we'll-talk-about-this-more-later face and smiles without showing any teeth. I don't want to talk about it now, and I won't want to talk about it later. Talking about feelings is one of my mom's favorite things, but a lot of times I just can't talk about stuff. I write it down instead. I look like my mom on the outside; we're both tall and sorta skinny with blue eyes and straight brown hair. But inside I'm quieter, like my dad.

Taylor pulls me off my stool. "Science test tomorrow, remember?"

My head nods and my feet follow her, but my stomach still feels like it's down near my feet doing flips and flops, and my head is starting to sweat. And this is only the beginning of what would happen if I actually tried to stand up in front of our class and do or say anything.

Taylor and I escape up the stairs to my room. I flop across my bed one way; Taylor flops the other. I close my eyes and concentrate on breathing. It's easier to concentrate with my eyes closed. Because when they're open, all I see is pink. My room looks like someone came in and threw up pink everywhere. The carpet is pink, the walls are pink and the comforter on my bed is pink. Even the curtains around both windows are pink.

My mom thinks I should love it. I don't. I don't like pink. I never have. I never liked princesses or ballerinas either. I like anything with polka dots, reading books, and collecting words. The only thing in my room that makes it feel like it's actually mine is the bookshelf crammed full of my books. My mom said we can redecorate when I turn twelve. My birthday is in November. I'm counting the days. Today makes 228.

"Do you really want to study for science now?" I ask. "Because if you want, you could go back and talk to my mom some more." I give her my squinty eyes look. This time—finally—she gets it.

"I'm sorry. But you know I lose my mind when I eat her pizza." So not an excuse. "But hey, now you've got a great idea for your project. You can do a scrapbook." Taylor doesn't even finish talking before she bursts out laughing. "You know what they say, 'A picture is worth a thousand words.'" And she's off laughing again.

"Oh, shut up." I swat her with my pillow. I can't help but laugh, too. "But wait, what did you say?"

"You should do a scrapbook?"

"No, the part after that," I say.

"A picture is worth a thousand words?" Taylor's scrunched up face means she's not following me.

"Yeah."

"Not sure I get that, but okay."

Taylor and I worked on science until her mom picked her up, which was right before my mom asked me to set the table for dinner. And now, after dinner, it's the same as every night. My mom helps Daisy with her bath while my dad packs our lunches for tomorrow. I'm supposed to be finishing up my homework. I'm not. Instead, I keep thinking about what Taylor said about a picture being worth a thousand words.

I plop down on the floor in front of my bookshelf. In the middle of the bottom shelf are the hardcover *Charlotte's Web* I got for my seventh birthday, the book of saints that was my mom's when she was a kid, and my collection of Curious George stories. Daisy says I should give Curious George to her—which is so *not* happening. And behind Charlotte, the saints, and George hides a notebook. It looks like an ordinary school notebook. It's not.

Some people, like Taylor, collect stuffed animals. Grandma and Grandpa Humphrey collect magnets from all fifty states—their fridge is covered. But me, I collect words. I love to learn new words and find words that mean exactly the right thing or that feel fun in my mouth. Words like stupendous, persnickety and frankfurter. I like words that sound like what they mean—like scintillating, thwack and shimmer. And I've written them all down, in this notebook.

I flip through the pages and smile at how big and sometimes crooked the letters are on the first bunch of pages. That was second grade. I watch my handwriting get smaller and neater, and roll my eyes when I come to last year's pages where every lowercase *i* or *j* was dotted with a heart. Page after page filled with words. I keep going until I find a blank page, take the scrap paper out of my pocket, and copy down today's word: *conundrum*—a puzzling question or problem. Yep. The perfect word for today, and maybe even for that day in second grade Madison never lets me forget.

I started my collection when I was in second grade. I used to carry it around in a special tote bag and show it to people. And one day I stood up to share it with my entire second grade class. Only I never actually got to tell everyone about it. Because it turns out I get really nervous when a bunch of people are staring at me, waiting for me to say something. And that time when I got really nervous, I froze. *All of me* was so frozen I didn't notice what was happening until the kids in the front of the class started pointing and laughing. And then Madison Marinelli shouted, "Look. It's a puddle." And there was a puddle . . . right where I was standing.

That was the first time Madison Marinelli called me Puddles; but not the last time. It *was* the last time I stood up in front of the class and did anything. And I never shared my word collection with anyone again. Nobody—not even my mom or Taylor—knows I'm still doing it.

Could my words somehow be my self-portrait? Maybe.

But it doesn't matter because I'm not going to get up in front of the class.

I won't.

I can't.

word #985

discombobulated

confused or disconcerted

Jack Quinn is wearing cologne—a lot of cologne. That's new. And that's the first thing I notice as I walk to class. The second thing is that I have to walk past Madison and Addison to get there. As always, they look as much like one and the same person as possible. I'm just not sure who that person is.

We wear navy blue and white uniforms, so we all look kind of alike. But Madison and Addison take it even further and wear matching socks, shoes and headbands. They have straight hair that is parted on the left side and rests precisely on their shoulders. Madison's hair is the exact color of peanut butter—creamy not crunchy. Addison is Korean American and has shiny black hair. Somehow the matching sneers on their faces make them look more identical than you'd think they could.

They're standing at Madison's locker, taking turns looking in her mirror. I tell myself that they won't notice me walk by and I feel my shoulders relax. Too soon. At the exact same time, they spin around and look at me—stare really—from the top of my head down to my shoes. Then Addison whispers something to Madison. The only word I can make out is Puddles. Then they crack up and turn back around.

I take a deep breath and open my mouth, hoping something really good will come out, something that will shut them up for once. For good, even. But nothing comes out. Not one word. So, I continue on to class and drop into my seat.

I know it's smarter to ignore them. That's what teachers and parents and everyone always says. But, here's the thing: ignoring them seems like letting them win. They're horrible to everyone—all the girls in our class and most of the boys, too.

Again, Taylor arrives at the exact moment the morning bell rings. I don't know how she does that. Right behind her is Mr. Summer with a girl who looks like she could be a fifth grader. She's wearing a St. Joe's uniform. The brightness of the colors announces that it's brand new. But the girl looks miserable.

"Class," says Mr. Summer. "This is Lacey Cavanaugh. Her family just moved here from Ohio. I know you'll make her feel welcome." A new student in our class? We haven't had a new student since Abby Fogelman showed up at the beginning of second grade. And some of the kids were still calling her "the new girl" last year. I look around and see that everyone is staring at Lacey like she's an animal in the zoo. I glance back at Lacey. She's staring at a spot over all of our heads. Her knees are popping—lock, unlock, lock, unlock.

Mr. Summer tells Lacey to take the desk next to Jack and in front of me.

I scribble a note to Taylor that says, *Tay—Worst thing ever to be new now! Wanna ask her to eat lunch with us?—A.*

I pass the note behind me to Taylor. And notice that Mr. Summer has stopped talking about verb tenses. I look up to see him staring at me. He puts his hand out and says, "Annie?"

He doesn't need to say anything else. Mr. Summer has a policy about passing notes. He takes them and reads them to the class.

I take the note and hand it to him. "Sorry, Mr. Summer."

He reads the note and says, "Lacey, it seems that Annie and her friend Taylor want you to have lunch with them today. Is that okay with you?"

Lacey glances up at me and almost smiles before she looks back down at her desk. "I guess," she says.

"Well, now that we've settled that, can we get back to our verbs please?" asks Mr. Summer. He smiles at me so I know he's not annoyed.

"Teacher's pet," hisses Madison. Of course that's what she would think. It would never occur to one of them to do something nice. It doesn't matter, though. It'll be fun to get to know Lacey— and maybe make a new friend.

"It must be really hard for you to have to change schools when it's almost the end of the year." I don't want to be nosy, but I'm not always the best at small talk. That's Taylor's area. And she's in line buying her lunch. I investigate the contents of today's nutritious lunch, packed by my dad, while I wait for Lacey to answer.

"Yeah, it's hard. No offense, but I don't want to be here," says Lacey. She looks like she's going to cry. Lacey's wavy, red hair and the freckles on her nose make her look like someone who might be friendly. Right now she just looks like someone trying not to cry.

"Um, I'm sorry." Lacey doesn't answer. She just keeps staring at the table while a tear drips off the end of her nose and plops onto the table.

I scramble for a way to make this better. "Our school and Mr. Summer are pretty nice. And Glenville's an okay place to live. It's kinda small—well, some people think it's really small—but I like it." Ugh. When I get nervous, I sometimes start to babble. And once I start, it's hard to stop. Oh good, here comes Taylor. Finally.

"Hey! Well, it's fish sticks day. This isn't going to be good. I hope your dad packed enough to share." I pass Taylor half of my turkey and cheese sandwich. She sits down and smiles her huge smile. Then she sees the look on Lacey's face. "Geez Annie, I was only gone for a minute. What did you say to make her cry?" I think she's kidding, but I'm not sure. Either way, she didn't need to say it.

"I didn't make her cry," I say. "I just asked a question. You do the talking then." I crunch on a carrot stick.

"It's not Annie's fault," Lacey says. "I just moved away from the only school I've ever gone to and all my friends. Now I'm here where I don't know anyone. It totally stinks."

"Agreed. Totally stinks," says Taylor. "Why'd you have to move?" she asks around a bite of her half of my sandwich. I don't know why I worried about seeming nosy. Taylor won't stop until she gets the whole story.

"My dad lost his job. And while he was trying to find a new one, my mom found a new one for herself instead. Here. In Michigan." Lacey bites her lip and blinks a bunch of times. "And my dad hasn't come yet. And no one will tell me why. I tried to get them to leave me behind with him so that I could at least finish the school year in Ohio at my own school with my own friends. But my mom said no. That's all. Just no. So here I am." Only now does Lacey take a breath . . . a shaky one.

"Okay. That does stink. A lot. But now that you're here, maybe Annie and I can help it stink less." And again she smiles her Taylor smile. This time, Lacey can't help but smile back a little.

"Go ahead and try," says Lacey.

"Okay, tell us one weird thing about you," Taylor says. This is one of her favorite games.

"Weird, huh?" says Lacey. She thinks for a minute. "Well, I have exactly seventeen freckles on my face. In the summer, they'll multiply until there're about a gazillion of them. But by Halloween, I'll count them again and it'll be back to seventeen. Every year, back to seventeen." And for the first time, she smiles a real smile.

We spend the rest of lunch swapping stories and sharing information. Lacey likes to read and draw and listen to music. I love to read, and Taylor and I both like music, too. We talk about the self-portrait project and Lacey already thinks she knows what she's going to do. And she's only been here for half a day. I still have no idea what I'm going to do and I've been here forever.

Only one thing comes close to ruining lunch. As we stand up and start to head out for recess, Madison and Addison come over. Madison leans over and whispers in my ear, "She's not going to want to be *your* friend." And they walk away. Lacey looks at me like she's wondering what's going on. I shrug and don't say anything. I don't know how to even start explaining them to Lacey. She'll figure it out herself before long.

The science test is after recess. It's on the parts of the cell—like the cell wall and the cell membrane and the nucleus. I do okay on the written part, but then there's a part where we have to look at slides under a microscope and identify what we're looking at. And worst of all, we have to draw a cell and label its parts. Even though I studied and got help from Taylor, I can tell it's not going well. Nothing I look at under the microscope looks like anything that was in the book. I see squiggles and blobs. And I know these squiggles and blobs are supposed to be something. But I have no idea what that something is. Sigh. Science is going to be my worst grade for the rest of my life.

After we turn in our tests, Mr. Summer wants to talk about our project. "Any questions about the Fifth Farewell?" he asks. "Does anyone want to share their ideas yet?"

"Do we have to do it?" asks Sam Brewer. Everybody laughs. Sam is only serious when it's about baseball.

Sam turns and grins at me. Before I can smile back, I feel my face get hot and my stomach does a weird sinking thing like when I ride a roller coaster. I don't like roller coasters. I look down at my desk and tuck my hair behind my ears. Twice. What was that?

Sam lives across the street from me; I can't remember a time when I didn't know him. My mom has a bunch of completely embarrassing pictures of us from when we were babies—in a scrapbook, of course. Sam was super-chubby and always chewing on things, including me. And I was completely bald.

We used to play all kinds of games and spend entire afternoons exploring our backyards, looking for bugs or four-leaf clovers. We've always been the only "same age" kids on our street. But when Sam turned nine, his mom started letting him ride his bike two streets over to Jalen and Trevor's houses. So now he mostly hangs out with the two of them, playing baseball, slugging each other, and having burping contests. Sometimes all at the same time.

"Yes Sam, you do have to complete the assignment," says Mr. Summer. "Are there any questions about the actual project?"

"Why is called a farewell?" asks Lacey.

"Can anyone answer that?" Mr. Summer loves to make us answer each other's questions.

Jalen pokes me in the back. When I don't say anything, he starts talking. "Well, it's a tradition, which I guess means some old guy thought it was a good idea a really long time ago." Most of the class laughs and Mr. Summer clears his throat and gives Jalen a "warning" look. "Okay, it's because we're leaving the little kid school. Next year we'll be all the way on the other side of the church starting middle school." Without turning around, I can hear the shrug in Jalen's voice. "It's just a St. Joe thing. It always has been. And I guess that makes it kind of important."

Mr. Summer nods and smiles one of his proud-of-one-of-us smiles. "Any other questions?"

Jenna Martinez raises her hand. "Does it have to be a real picture, like taken with a camera? Can I draw something instead?" She looks as confused about this as I feel. And she's the super-brain of our class. That makes me feel a little better.

"No, not at all," says Mr. Summer. "I want each of you to use your imagination and come up with something that is a reflection of you. It *can* be a picture or a drawing, but it doesn't have to be that literal. Just be creative and make sure that whatever you do represents who you are."

Well, thanks for clearing that up. I think I might be more confused than I was. I look around the room and see I'm not the only one. Trevor Blonski is scratching his head and Oliver Stephenson's mouth is hanging open like he doesn't even know what question to ask.

"Mr. Summer, I'm going to make a video with a bunch of pictures of me," says Madison, with what I hate to admit is an impressive hair flip. "It would be too hard to pick just one." I think she's serious.

Taylor and I roll our eyes at each other and Taylor giggles. Madison turns and glares at her. Then she picks up her books and slinks to the door. Madison has been getting extra help in the Resource Room for as long as I can remember. And she's been trying to sneak out of the room to do it as long as I can remember, too. I don't know why she bothers—everybody knows and nobody cares. If you need extra help, you get it. No big deal.

"Well, it sounds like you have some interesting ideas. Go with them. It's up to each of you to decide your approach. That's the fun of this assignment," says Mr. Summer.

So, this project is supposed to be fun? Good to know. I'm still discombobulated about what I'm going to do—or how to get out of doing it at all—and about how not to fail science. That might have to be my word for today. *Discombobulated*.

word #986

effervescent

bubbling, lively, and sparkling

The houses on my street look like farmhouses without their farms. Ours is white with green shutters and it has a long front porch with a swing. My mom says it's perfect for sitting and watching the neighborhood go by. It's her favorite-in-all-the-world spot. Not me.

When I was six, my dad built a bench for me under the enormous oak tree in our backyard. It's my oasis—where I escape to read, think, or sometimes just get away from Daisy. When I need privacy or quiet, this is where I come. I love that my dad made it for me. We don't talk about everything and he doesn't ask me a ton of questions like my mom does, but he gets what I need—like this spot.

My back resting against the tree, I pull my knees up under my chin, close my eyes and wait. Maybe, if I sit here long enough, a brilliant idea will find its way to my brain and I'll figure out a solution to my Fifth Farewell problem. Or even a not-so-brilliant idea that will save me from standing up in front of my class and having something utterly humiliating happen—again.

I stay there so long that my right foot falls asleep. The only thing that feels like it might be an idea is using my word collection. I'm up to 984 words. My only plan right now is to hope that when I get to 1,000 words, I'll know what to do. As plans go, it's not a good one.

The screen door slaps closed and I look up to see Taylor trudging across the backyard. I didn't know she was coming over.

"What's wrong?" I ask. Her usual smile is missing and her shoulders are slumped. Even her curls look like they've lost their bounce.

"Only everything," she says. "I'm not having a birthday party this year. I'm hardly even having a birthday." Taylor slumps down next to me and starts to cry. Taylor almost never cries.

"What do you mean? You always have a party," I say.

Taylor turns eleven next weekend and she has been counting down the days to her party. Her mom is even more creative than Taylor, so her parties are always super fun and original.

"Not this year. This year's different. Everything's different," says Taylor. She cries even harder. "Because of everything with Zach, my mom said that she doesn't have the energy to plan a party. I asked if we could at least go out to dinner and she said no. Zach had a big meltdown the last time we went out to eat because it was loud and crowded, and now he's even on some special diet one of the doctors told her to try. And you know my mom doesn't cook, so I can't even have a special birthday dinner at home like your mom always makes for you. So I guess I'm not having a birthday at all."

"I'm so sorry. I didn't know. What can I do?" I have no idea how to make her feel better.

"Nothing," says Taylor. "There's nothing anyone can do. Everything is about Zach now. My mom keeps asking me to be patient and to be understanding. But it's my *birthday*. I don't want to be patient or understanding about my birthday. I thought I could at least have this one day."

Taylor swipes at her tears and tries to smile. It's not convincing. "I'll be okay," she says. "I just don't want to talk about it anymore." She hiccups from crying which makes us laugh. I reach over and give her a sideways hug. I don't know what else to do or say. For now, changing the subject seems like the right thing to do.

"Okay. We won't talk about it. Did I tell you Lacey and I have plans to hang out this weekend while you're gone?" I say. Taylor and her family are going to visit her grandparents.

"You are? I guess that could be fun," says Taylor. She's quiet for a minute and then bolts to her feet and spins around to face me. "Promise me you won't tell her about Zach. I don't want her to know," she says. "Promise."

"Of course I won't tell her," I say. "I promise." It hurts that she feels like she needs to tell me that. Taylor doesn't want anyone to know Zach has autism. I know that. She sits back down and relaxes into the tree.

"But Lacey's nice, don't you think? And fun, too," I say. Taylor and I have had lunch with Lacey every day at school.

"She's okay, I guess. I'm sick of hearing about how terrible it is to be here though, and I know more about Ohio than I ever wanted to—that's all she ever talks about," says Taylor.

"I know. I'm sure it'll get better after she gets used to it. She'll figure out it's not so bad," I say. Taylor shrugs. I'm excited about having a new friend. I don't think Taylor is, but I'm sure she'll change her mind.

One sniff tells me we're having spaghetti and meatballs for dinner. The kitchen smells like an Italian restaurant—all garlic and spices.

I slide onto a stool at the counter next to Daisy and sigh a sigh that comes from my toes.

"What's wrong, honey?" My mom stops stirring the sauce, puts down her wooden spoon, and looks me right in the eye. My mom is a great listener. Sometimes this is a good thing.

"It's actually Taylor's problem. You know how it's her birthday next week?" My mom nods. "Well, because of all the stuff with Zach, her mom said she can't have a party this year and they won't even take her out to dinner or anything. Taylor was crying about it this afternoon. And I don't know what to do to help."

"Poor Taylor," says my mom. "This is such a hard time for her family."

"I know, Mom, but it's Taylor's birthday. Shouldn't she still get a special day?" I ask.

"Well honey, it sounds like her mom's not going to be able to give her a party this year," my mom says. "Try to understand."

"We can give Taylor a party!" Daisy bounces up and down.

"What do you mean?" I say.

"We can have a birthday party for Taylor here. I can help you plan it and everything," says Daisy. She hops off her stool. "We can make a cake and have pizza and play games and dance!" And she twirls around the kitchen, her tutu flaring out with every spin.

"That's a good idea," says my mom. "I can make the pizzas, and we'll have cake and ice cream. You girls can decide who else to invite and what to do for fun. I'll call Mrs. Matthews right now and make sure it's okay with her."

I try not to mind that Daisy came up with the perfect idea for helping Taylor. But the truth is I kind of do mind. Daisy is my little sister. And since she's only in first grade, it seems like I should be the one with the answers. Instead, I follow her out of the kitchen, trying to keep up. Daisy chatters almost as fast as she twirls.

My mom is always telling me how she was a late bloomer. It seems like she's trying to reassure me that I will bloom one day. But Daisy already blooms. Sometimes I catch myself wishing I was more like my little sister. That seems kind of backward—isn't she supposed to want to be like me?

word #987

juxtapose

to put side by side for comparison or contrast

Lacey's house is on the other side of the park from mine, so I take the path that cuts through instead of going around. Tall trees line one side of the path, keeping the sun from feeling too hot. A baseball game is just getting started on the field. A baseball game probably means Sam. And there he is, blond hair sticking out from the back of his cap. I see him right before he spots me. And he sees me at the exact moment I trip over a sticking-up-tree-root and barely keep from falling on my face. Sam yells "Hey, Annie," as he settles under a pop-fly, catching it easily. I wave and keep walking.

Clumsy. Ever since I started feeling weird about Sam, I've been clumsy. I don't have any experience with boys, but I'm pretty sure clumsy isn't the way to get noticed . . . at least not in a good way.

I hear a voice yell, "Moose! Stop! Come back!" and see a kind of small, really ugly dog coming my way. There's a leash attached to the dog but no person attached to the other end of the leash.

"Sit, Moose," I say. The dog stops and plops its butt down on my foot. I laugh.

"Moose!" yells a voice from further down the path. I know that voice. And here's the boy who goes with the voice. It's Oliver from school. His face is red and his brown hair is sticking up even more than just his usual cowlick. He sees me, stops, and reaches down to pick up the other end of the leash.

"Annie, hi. So you met Moose. He got away from me."

"I heard. And saw." I reach down and pet Moose. "He's so cute."

"No he's not," says Oliver, the dimple in his cheek flashing. "He's a really ugly dog. Don't worry though, he doesn't mind."

I look closer. "Okay, so he's not cute. But he's so not-cute that somehow he ends up being cute," I say.

Oliver laughs.

We talk for a few minutes about dogs and our Fifth Farewell projects. Oliver's as stumped as I am about what to do. At least it's not just me.

"I don't know," I say. "I had an idea this morning but it's not exactly a plan yet. And I'm not even sure if it's a good idea, anyway."

"Yeah?" Oliver reaches down and gets a tiny stick. He tosses it to Moose who runs over and starts wrestling with it. We both laugh.

"Hey, do you still have your word collection?" asks Oliver.

"What?" How does he know about my collection?

"Remember? You showed it to all of us in second or third grade." Oliver scratches his elbow. "I don't remember which."

"It was second." I can't forget.

"It was so cool."

"Really? You thought it was cool?"

"I started my own collection after that," Oliver says. "But I only collected words that started with 'z.'"

"Why only 'z'?"

"I don't remember. I think I just liked the way they sounded. *Zoom, zoinks, zip, zing, zoo, zesty.*" Oliver ticks the words off on his fingers as he goes.

"*Zamboni,*" I say.

Oliver's eyebrows go way up. "Zamboni?"

I shrug. "My dad likes hockey."

"Cool." Oliver pretends to take a slap shot. "Hey, do you still have your collection? Because you could totally use that. It would be awesome."

I stare at Oliver for a long time. Nothing about his face says he's making fun of me. But doesn't he remember?

"Don't you remember what happened the last time?" I say. And that's all I say. I don't mention anything about how when I got up to share my collection with the class, I got so nervous and scared that I couldn't talk. Or feel most of the parts of my body. How I just stood there, clutching my notebook. And peeing on the floor.

"It was a long time ago. What happened?"

He really doesn't remember? It was the single most embarrassing moment of my entire life and Oliver doesn't remember? Could that mean some of the other kids don't remember either? Or if they do, they don't care?

"Anyway, I'm sure whatever your idea is, it's great. I know it's better than my idea since I don't have one." Oliver shrugs and laughs a little.

"Well, I'd better get going to Lacey's," I say. "See you Monday."

"See ya," says Oliver. "Oh, and Moose says 'bye' and 'it was nice meeting you.'"

I laugh and walk in the direction of Lacey's house. Oliver is nice and easy to talk to. I managed to have a whole conversation with him without tripping or saying something stupid.

When I come out of the park onto Mulvaney Street, it looks like I'm not in the same town. The houses on Lacey's street are smaller and all of them are one story and red brick. They line the street like soldiers. At first they all look alike. But when I look a little closer, I notice one has blue shutters and another has a front door with a stained glass window. When I get to the address Lacey told me, I walk up the sidewalk and ring the doorbell.

Sharp. That's the word that pops into my head when Mrs. Cavanaugh opens the front door. Everything about her is sharp. She's so thin I can see the bones in her face. Her nose and chin are pointy. And she doesn't look like it's Saturday morning. She's wearing pants and a blouse— perfectly ironed with sharp creases.

When she speaks, that's sharp too. "Yes? What is it?"

"Hi," I say. "I'm Annie. Annie Humphrey. Is Lacey home?" I start to smile, but that doesn't seem like the right thing to do because she's not smiling so I stop.

"Hello, Annie. Lacey didn't say anything about having company," says Mrs. Cavanaugh.

I tuck my hair behind my ears, do it again, and open my mouth to say something . . . anything. Nothing comes out so I think about leaving. Before I can, Lacey comes up behind her mom.

"Hey, Annie! Come on in," she says.

I can't. Her mom is still standing in the doorway and she's not moving.

"Lacey, you didn't tell me you were having company," Mrs. Cavanaugh says.

"Nope, I didn't," says Lacey. "Come on, Annie." And she reaches around her mom and pulls me into the house. Awkward.

"Is it okay that I'm here?" I ask Lacey once we're in her room.

"Yeah, why wouldn't it be?" she asks. "Oh, you mean because of my mom. It's fine. Don't worry about her."

"Okay." This feels weird, but I don't ask any more questions. "I like your room. You'd never know you just moved in," I say. It's true. There's not a box in sight or a thing out of place. It doesn't look like an eleven-year-old girl lives in it.

"No way do you like my room. My mom decorated it like it's a guest room for an old person. I'm hoping it means we're not staying," says Lacey.

She has a point about the old person thing. All of the colors are what my mom calls 'restful' and there are no posters or bulletin boards or pictures of friends. There's just a big picture on the wall. It's a vase of flowers. My Grandma Humphrey has one like it in her living room. Maybe my pink-explosion room isn't so bad.

"Okay, I was being polite. It's pretty. It just doesn't look like a kid's room," I say. Then I spy something that makes me forget all about grandma-looking paintings and a too-neat bed. "Oh, look at all your books."

Lacey has a long bookcase under her window that's filled with books—all arranged very neatly, of course. It has a cushion on top where Lacey could sit and read and still see out the window. I flop down on the rug and start looking through her titles.

"Oh, *Little Women* is my favorite book ever! And *Anne of Green Gables*. Oh, and the *Little House* books and *Charlotte's Web*. We have the same collection," I say.

"We do? I love all of these and so many more. But I only keep my total favorites," says Lacey. "Who's your favorite character in *Little Women*?" Well, this started out shaky, but it's getting better.

"Jo, of course. Isn't Jo everyone's favorite? I always want to be like her, brave and strong. And I like Meg. Beth just makes me cry. How about you? Who's your favorite?" I ask. It's great to have a friend to talk to about books. Taylor doesn't get what reading means to me. It's words. A good book is the perfect words used perfectly.

"Well my favorite character ever is Anne Shirley. You know, red hair and freckles." Lacey twirls a hunk of her own red hair. She laughs. "And I always wished I lived at Green Gables. But in *Little Women*, it's Marmee," says Lacey. "Marmee is my favorite. She's kind of like my mom used to be."

I don't know what to say. I just met Lacey's mom, and she didn't seem anything like the mom in *Little Women*, that's for sure.

"Ever since she decided we were moving here, my mom's been acting like the ice queen. She even changed her name. Well, sort of. She's always been Maggie. But now she introduces herself to everyone as Margaret, like she's someone else." Lacey chews on her lip. "My dad calls her Meg. Or at least he used to. Sometimes if I want to make her mad, I call her Marge. I make her mad a lot. Even when I'm not trying to," Lacey says. And she laughs, but not the kind of laugh like something's funny. The kind like it's not.

"Why do you want to make her mad?" I ask.

"Because I had to leave everything and every-one I cared about and come live here in this old lady room. And she never even said she was sorry. And my dad's not here yet and no one will say when he's coming." Lacey stares out the window for so long I think she forgets I'm here.

"Hey, do you want to go to the park?" I ask. I need to get out of this house. Lacey seems like a different person here. Part of me is gladder than ever that I'm trying to be her friend. She needs one.

"Sure, let's go," Lacey says. "Forget what I said about my mom."

I'll try, but I don't think I can. We don't see Mrs. Cavanaugh on the way out. Lacey and I go to the park and walk around. She seems lighter somehow after we get away from her house. We hop on the swings and see who can swing higher. By the time you're in fifth grade, it's not cool to go on the swings at recess. That doesn't mean it's not still fun.

Then we lie on our stomachs on our swings and spin in slow circles. Sometimes it's easier for me to talk when I don't have to look at the person I'm talking to. "I had an idea for my project."

"You did? What is it?" asks Lacey. Her hair looks like a red curtain, sweeping the ground under her swing as she twirls in one direction and then the other.

"You know how we were talking about our favorite characters? Well, I thought that maybe I could do something like a character profile. You know, like you do for a book report," I say. It sounded like a good idea in my head this morning, now I'm not sure.

"Hmm," says Lacey. "Then you can talk about yourself as the main character of your own story." She stops her swing with the toe of her shoe and looks up at me. "That's a great idea. And perfect for you."

I shrug because it doesn't really matter what idea I have for my project. Puddles is not standing up in front of the class and doing anything. And not for the first time, I wonder what happens if a St. Joe's fifth grader doesn't do a Fifth Farewell. Could they make me do fifth grade again?

"I've been working on my painting. I hope it's ready in time," says Lacey.

"What is it?" I ask. Lacey told us she used to take private art lessons before she moved here. I can't wait to see what she does.

"You'll have to wait and see with everyone else," Lacey says. "I'm not showing anyone ahead of time."

"That's fair." I glance at my watch. "Hey, I need to get going. I told my mom I'd be home for lunch. I'll walk you home." I get up from my swing. There's a minute of the weird feeling you get when the world comes back to being right side up. Things look new and different.

Lacey and I walk back to her house. We say bye and I watch Lacey walk up to her front door. She takes a breath so deep I can see it, balls her fists like she's ready for a fight and opens the door.

This time I take the long way home. When I get there, I find my mom and hug her. She looks surprised but doesn't ask any questions. I wouldn't know what to say if she did.

word #988

trepidation

a condition of anxiety or dread; alarm

"My mom asked if we wanted to invite any boys to your party," I say. "I said no, but I guess I should've asked you first. Do you want boys there?"

"No way," says Taylor without hesitating.

"At my old school, we started having boy/girl parties this year," says Lacey. "Some kids even coupled up. I didn't, but there was one boy I thought was cute." She looks across the playground toward the kickball field. A bunch of the kids in our class play every day. "You know, there are some cute boys in our class."

"Like who?" asks Taylor.

Lacey looks around to make sure no one is close enough to hear. "Well, Sam for sure. And Jack's kinda cute too."

My stomach does a flip when she says Sam's name. I push my hair back behind my ears and stare at the ground without saying anything.

"Cute? Jack sucked his thumb until the middle of third grade and Sam spent last year farting in class to make the other boys laugh," says Taylor. "Nobody's cute enough to make me forget that kind of stuff." She laughs, but I know what she means.

"So, no boys," I say.

"No boys." Taylor shakes her head hard enough to send her hair flying. "What I want to know is why you won't tell me what we're doing or what we're having to eat?"

My mom and I thought it would be fun to keep the details secret from Taylor. It's driving her crazy. We were right. It is fun.

"Just be at my house by five o'clock on Saturday. That's all you need to know. Oh, and Daisy says you're supposed to wear something festive."

"I hope she doesn't mean a tutu or a princess dress." Taylor curtsies low. Too low. She clutches my arm to keep from toppling over.

"It's possible. We're talking Daisy," I say.

"No tutu for me, but I'll need some fun after what my mom is making me do," says Lacey.

"Why? What is she making you do?" Lacey's still so mad at her mom, I'm almost afraid to ask.

"We have to go to dinner at her new boss's house Friday night. And guess who her new boss is?" Lacey asks.

"No idea," I say. Having dinner with your mom's boss doesn't sound super fun, but it can't be that bad.

"Madison's dad," she says.

"What? Seriously? Madison Marinelli's dad is your mom's new boss?" asks Taylor, her voice getting louder with each question.

"Yep," says Lacey. "Madison Marinelli's dad. I get to spend Friday night with Madison. Fun, huh?"

"Uh, no. Definitely not fun." I try to think of something to say to make Lacey feel better about this, but I can't. An evening with either of the two-headed amoeba sounds unbearable. But I suspect that Madison would be worse. She's usually the one who talks first. Wait, do amoebas even have heads?

"I tried to get out of it," says Lacey. "I even told my mom how mean Madison is to you guys . . . to everyone. But she said this is important for her new job, so 'I am to go with a smile on my face and be pleasant.'" Lacey sounds so much like her mom that I shiver. "My mom's big on being pleasant," she says with a fake smile. "I just need to make it till Saturday. Then we can have fun. I hope Madison isn't too awful."

As if Lacey conjures them up, here come Madison and Addison. They stop in front of us and look each of us up and down. After taking a minute to decide who today's victim will be, Madison speaks. "So Taylor, did you even bother to comb that mop on top of your head that you call hair? You really should make more of an effort." She looks at Addison for approval. They laugh and then start to walk away.

After a few steps, Madison stops and turns back around. "Hey, new girl. Didn't anyone tell you that you're hanging around with the losers? I mean, really—Puddles is your new friend? Poor new girl. Doesn't know any better," she says. She collects her other half and they prance away.

Lacey's right. I can't think of too many things worse than spending a Friday night with Madison Marinelli.

word #989

shindig

a party or dance

Daisy and I race to open the front door. I win. "Happy Birthday!" I say, okay shriek, and hug Taylor.

"I'm so excited!" says Taylor. "Thank you, thank you, thank you for giving me a party!" Her smile is as bright as her T-shirt—electric blue with sparkles.

"Yes, thank you, Annie. And you too, Daisy." Mrs. Matthews looks tired and like she has to work at smiling. Still, she's here and that's what matters.

"Come on, Taylor. I want to show you everything." Daisy grabs Taylor by the hand and drags her out the back door, trailing ribbons behind her. Daisy decorated her pink tutu with construction paper flowers and tied on a bunch of the kind of ribbon Mom uses to wrap presents. She even made a crown of plastic flowers for her hair. Definitely festive. Definitely Daisy.

The party's in our backyard. Daisy said there had to be a theme and, after convincing her that a princess party wasn't the way to go, we settled on flowers. Taylor loves flowers—big, bright, bold flowers that match her personality. So, it's a Taylor-style garden party.

As promised, Daisy was in charge of decorations. Masses of balloons bob in the breeze, and confetti shaped like flowers covers the tables and benches. Earlier today, my dad helped Daisy hang streamers from tree branches and she made a giant poster with a number 11 made from glitter. Taylor walks outside, spins in a circle to see it all and squeals.

We dig into some of the munchies my mom set out. Because she can't help herself, she snuck in healthy ones wherever she could. There are also little flowerpots—one for each guest and an extra one for my dad—filled with some type of Oreo cookie and chocolate pudding mixture that looks like dirt and has gummy worms coming out of it. Daisy and Taylor love them. I think they look disgusting.

The doorbell rings again. This time it's Jenna and Abby from our class. Jenna and Abby are crazy about singing—they're both in the St. Joe's honors chorus. It's usually only for middle school kids and they're only in fifth grade. They sing all the time and have to go to extra practices a lot, sometimes even during lunch and recess. Still, they're fun to have around. Jenna and Abby start giggling and munching with Taylor.

Now we're only waiting for Lacey. I hope she gets here soon.

We dance around the backyard. My dad is in charge of music as long as he only plays the songs I gave him (which means nothing embarrassing from when he was a kid and nothing he might want to dance to). So far, so good.

Sweaty and out of breath from dancing, I'm looking for something to drink when my mom calls me over to where she is standing with Mrs. Matthews.

"What's up?" I ask.

"It's almost 6:00, honey, and Lacey still isn't here. Since she's so late, do you want to wait for her or go ahead and eat?"

"I didn't know it was that late. I'll go call her and see if she's still coming," I tell my mom. "I guess we should have the pizza now. Everyone's probably hungry."

"Okay, I'll get everything ready." My mom heads for the kitchen to set out five different kinds of pizza—I hope she saves me a slice of the four cheese and tomato. I grab the phone and duck into the hall. I dial Lacey's number and wait for someone to answer. No one does. I leave a message and hang up.

Weird. Lacey was excited about Taylor's party and told me after school yesterday that she'd see us today. I hope nothing bad happened.

My mom has magical powers. She has to. How else could she transform the picnic table that was overflowing with pizza crusts, cups of crazy-bright pink punch, plates and napkins into a sort of art studio?

"Everyone gets a canvas, paints, some yarn and a bowl full of buttons," I say. This project was my idea. Taylor loves to do crafts. But this is easy enough for all of us to do, even Daisy. "You can decide what to make—like a tree or a row of flowers. Oh, and my mom will help us with the hot glue."

"A house. I'm making a house," Daisy bounces up and down.

"Wait. So what am I supposed to do? What am I supposed to make?" Jenna's voice gets higher and louder.

"Whatever you want," I say. "Just kind of lay out what you want to do and then glue it down. It's fun."

I can't quite decide if I want to make a rainbow or a bouquet. My mom must have emptied out her button collection because there are buttons in every size and color imaginable.

Taylor and Abby sit down and get right to work. After my mom covers Daisy from her nose to her toes in an old shirt of my dad's, she gets started, too. But not Jenna.

"Seriously, what am I supposed to do?" There's a line between her eyebrows. And she's fidgeting in her seat.

"Just make something," I tell her. "It'll be fine."

"But, I don't know what to do," Jenna says, whispers really, and then stops talking. She sits with her hands folded in her lap.

My mom comes and puts her hands on Jenna's shoulders. "Jenna, there's no wrong way to do this. What's your favorite color?"

Jenna ponders my mom's question for a long time. It's a simple question. "Um, I guess it's purple. No yellow." Her hand reaches out and flutters between the two piles of buttons. "No, it's purple." She nods her head like she's trying to convince herself.

Jenna looks up at my mom, frown still in place. My mom squeezes her shoulders, leans over and whispers so only Jenna and I can hear, "There's no wrong way to do it, Jenna. Whatever you do will be just fine."

Finally, Jenna smiles. She takes a breath and gets started. I wonder if it's hard to be the smartest kid in class, the one who always gets everything right.

Taylor's picture turns out the best. She made actual flowers on it that look real except for the crazy colors she chose. And Jenna's turns out fine—better than fine really, just like my mom told her it would. She made a tree with leaves in all different colors. After staring at it for a long time, a smile flashes across her face. I think she's happy with it.

"Hey Annie, where's Lacey? Isn't she coming?" asks Taylor. We're getting ready to sing "Happy Birthday" and have cake and ice cream.

"I guess not. It's weird. She didn't call or anything. But hey, it's time for cake and then presents!"

When all the cleaning up is done and my mom is tucking Daisy into bed, I try to call Lacey again. This time someone finally answers. It's her mom.

"May I please speak with Lacey?" I ask.

"Who's calling?" asks Mrs. Cavanaugh.

"It's Annie. Annie Humphrey?" I say my name like it's a question. When Mrs. Cavanaugh doesn't say anything, I keep talking. "Lacey didn't come to the party at my house tonight—you know, the birthday party for our friend Taylor—and I wanted to make sure she was okay."

There's a pause. A really long pause. So long I start to wonder if we got disconnected. Then Mrs. Cavanaugh finally says, "It's late, Annie. Lacey can't come to the phone." And she hangs up without saying goodbye.

Late? It's only 8:30. This keeps getting weirder.

word #990

blindsided

attacked where a person is vulnerable

I didn't see Lacey in the hall and she's not in class yet either. The phone call with her mom after Taylor's party was weird and then Lacey didn't call me back yesterday. Still, part of me thinks it was just a misunderstanding. All of me hopes it was just a misunderstanding.

I hear Lacey's voice and look up in time to see her walk into the classroom. She's flipping her hair and giggling at something Sam and Jalen are saying. That's new. I don't think she's ever actually talked to Sam *or* Jalen. But that's not all that's new. Lacey looks different—really different. Her hair is parted on the left side and has been cut so it rests precisely on her shoulders. The waves are gone; each strand of hair on her head is ruler straight. And it's held off her face with a head-band. *The* headband. Other than the color, her hair looks the same as Madison and Addison's hair. And she's wearing new shoes—black ballet flats with little red bows, just like the ones Madison and Addison wear every day. What's going on?

Lacey sits down without looking at me or say-ing anything to me. As the bell rings and prayers and announcements start, I remember Taylor won't be here today. She has some kind of torture-filled, all day appointment at the orthodontist. My stomach flips and then flops in a way that makes me wish I'd skipped breakfast. This is not going to be a good day.

The morning creeps by. I can't concentrate on anything Mr. Summer is saying, so I have no idea what question he just asked me let alone what the answer is. I've been staring at the back of Lacey's new head trying to figure out what happened to her.

"Annie, are you with us this morning?" asks Mr. Summer. I am a good student. Even though I don't get perfect grades like Jenna, I always try my best. Mr. Summer knows this. Everyone knows this. And now everyone knows something is wrong.

"I'm sorry, Mr. Summer," I say. Madison and Addison whisper and laugh as I feel my face get redder and redder.

The morning finally ends. Great, lunch. Lunch without Taylor. And I'm guessing lunch without Lacey. I grab a book from my locker and shuffle in the direction of the cafeteria. Jenna and Abby wave as they head toward the music room.

Our usual table seems huge and quiet without Taylor and Lacey to keep me company. I unpack slowly and start on my turkey sandwich and apple. Taking tiny bites and chewing each one until it turns to mush doesn't take as long as I hope. I spend the rest of lunch pretending to read my book. It's impossible to concentrate since my eyes keep sliding away from the page to where Lacey sits whispering and laughing—with Madison and Addison.

On my way outside for recess, I slip into the girls' bathroom. There's Lacey, washing her hands and looking in the mirror. Checking out her new hair? Our eyes meet in the mirror for an instant before she looks away. She tries to walk past me without saying anything. I ask the question I've wanted to ask all morning.

"Lacey, what's going on?" I say. "Why'd you skip Taylor's party and why are you hanging out with *them*?"

Lacey says nothing. The door opens and Madison and Addison walk in.

"Come on, Lacey," says Addison. "We're going outside now. We have a lot to discuss. There's no one worth talking to in here." She giggles.

Madison looks at me with an even snottier look than usual. "Seriously Puddles, you thought Lacey wanted to be your friend? You're so boring and immature. Why would any girl want to be your friend when she could be our friend? You're so pathetic, it's funny." And she and her terrible friend laugh and laugh. I look at Lacey thinking she might finally say *something*, have some kind of explanation. She won't look at me and she doesn't say a word. Still, I hear her loud and clear.

I think I'm going to cry. Not because of what Madison said about me. I know it's not true—the immature part, anyway. My teachers' comments on my report cards always say how mature I am. And boring? Well, that's not true either. Is it? And they've been calling me Puddles for so long it hardly bothers me. What I'm trying not to cry about is Lacey.

I thought we were friends.

I leave the bathroom and start to walk toward the library to hide out for recess. But no, I won't give Lacey and her new friends a chance to think they scared me away. There's a pond on the far side of the playground where Sam and I used to look for frogs every day when we were in first grade. Since I don't have anything better to do, I walk around the kickball game that's just getting started and hope for some frogs to hang out with.

Something hits me in the back, hard. Really hard. So hard it knocks me to my hands and knees. I don't know what just happened, but it hurt. Bad.

A hand reaches down to help me up. It's Oliver. "Are you okay, Annie? The kickball hit you. Sam kicked it really hard and it went straight at you," he says. "It was a homerun. Oh no, you're bleeding."

This is bad. I look down and see that both of my hands and both of my knees are scraped raw. A trail of blood meanders its way down my leg toward my sock—one of my favorite red and white polka dot socks.

"Annie, are you okay?" Oliver asks again. I'm not. I'm just really not. I wipe the tears away as fast as I can. I nod and, without looking at him or any of the other kids who are standing in a not-far-enough-away circle staring at me, I get up and hobble back the way I came.

Sam yells, "Sorry, Annie. It was an accident." I don't turn around or answer. I can't.

I go inside and straight to the nurse's office. She is so kind and gentle that I have to blink to stop the tears from starting again. Once she cleans me up and gives me some band-aids for my knees, I have no reason to stay. I wish I could hide here until the end of the day.

By the time I get to class, everyone has been back from recess for a while and is doing their silent reading, or pretending to. I give Mr. Summer my late pass and walk stiffly to my seat. I don't look at anyone. As soon as I sit down, there it is. A poke in the middle of my back from Jalen. "You okay, Cupcake?"

"What?" I ask, without turning around.

"I asked if you're okay, *Cupcake*." He says the Cupcake part louder and slower this time. And now at least half the class is laughing.

"What are you talking about?"

Oh, no. As I ask the question, I remember something. Something that fills me with dread. Serious dread. Something that makes me wish I could disappear or that I had stayed home this morning. The something I'm remembering is that this morning I put on pink underpants with cupcakes on them. Cupcakes. Jalen—and everybody else—must have seen my underwear when I fell. I went down, but my skirt flew up.

This day can't get any worse, can it?

word #991

flabbergasted

overcome with surprise and bewilderment

My mom picks Daisy and me up after school and freaks out when I get in the car.

"Annie! What happened to you?"

It takes me a minute to figure out she means my scraped hands and knees and the bloodstains on my socks. I thought she had some kind of mom ESP and knew how rotten my day had been.

"Oh, it was a playground accident. I walked in front of a kickball. I'm fine." I try to laugh. The only thing that could make today worse would be my mom wanting to talk about it and about how I feel about all of it. She doesn't need to know what happened yet—or ever.

"Don't you want to go home to clean up and change?" she asks.

"No, I'm really fine and my knees stopped bleeding a while ago I have all the work Taylor missed today. I promised I'd bring it over right after school. Just drop me off at Taylor's, please, and I'll walk home."

The rest of the drive to Taylor's house is filled with Daisy's chatter about her day. Daisy had a great day.

Mrs. Matthews answers the door and tells me Taylor is in her room without ever looking at me. A commotion coming from the back of the house means Zach is in the middle of a meltdown. I limp up the stairs as fast as I can and knock on Taylor's door.

"If that's you, Mom, I'm still not talking to you."

"It's me."

"Come in."

I open the door and find Taylor sitting in her window seat staring out the window and hugging a pillow to her chest. She doesn't turn around. As much as my baby-girl-pink bedroom doesn't look like me, Taylor's is perfectly her. It's bright and colorful and almost always messy. The window seat has piles of cushions and pillows on it. It's the perfect place to sit and think and watch not much happen outside. I hop up next to Taylor and settle in, gently resting my chin on my scraped knees.

"I have your homework for you. You're so lucky you weren't in school today. It was the worst day ever. You won't believe what happened," I say.

"Really. Worst day ever, huh?"

"Yes. Get this. Lacey showed up with a new haircut and new shoes and is suddenly friends with Madison and Addison. She wouldn't talk to me at all and the other two were nastier than usual, if you can imagine that. It was really bad. Oh, and then I got hit by a kickball and fell down and got hurt. I ruined my favorite pair of socks and pretty much everyone saw my cupcake underwear. But can you believe Lacey? I thought she was our friend."

I notice that Taylor isn't saying anything, and that she doesn't look very interested, and that she still hasn't looked at me.

"Taylor? Is something wrong?" I ask. She turns her head and now, too late, I see that her eyes are red from crying.

"Yeah Annie, something's wrong. Everything is wrong. I actually have real problems. I had a bad day that didn't have anything to do with someone who was never a friend in the first place.

So yes, something is wrong." Taylor is trying not to cry. And she's angry. Really angry.

"What is it? Why are you so upset?" I sit up straight and try to touch her arm. She pulls away. She holds her pillow in front of her like a shield.

"Why am I so upset? Well, let me tell you a few of the things that made my day so special. First I spent hours at the orthodontist where some other doctor pulled two teeth and it hurt like crazy. And I was there by myself because my mom dropped me off and then took Zach to yet another doctor's appointment. I guess Zach had a hard time at the appointment because my mom forgot to come back and get me. Even though she promised me—and the nurse—she'd come right back. She didn't."

"She *forgot* you?" I ask.

"Yes, my mom actually forgot about me. I was sitting in the waiting room for two hours trying not to choke on bloody cotton balls while they tried to find someone to come get me. My mom wasn't answering her phone and my dad was in an important meeting. More important than me. They finally got a hold of my mom and she came back to get me, but not until after I threw up all over the waiting room. And she doesn't seem to be that sorry about forgetting me. She expects me to understand because Zach was having a problem. But *I* needed my mom, too." The last part comes out garbled and with a sob.

"I'm so sorry." Before I can say more, she starts again.

"So really, Annie I'm sorry if someone who didn't seem like she was that great turned out to be a fake. I didn't get why you wanted to be her friend so badly anyway. I guess it's not enough to just have me for a best friend," says Taylor.

"That's not true."

"I don't want to talk about it anymore," says Taylor. "Thanks for bringing my homework. I need to go find Zach. He wants to read his favorite dinosaur book with me again. I'll see you in school tomorrow." And she stands up, walks over and opens the door.

Is she kicking me out? Seriously?

"Okay. I'm really sorry," I say again.

We walk down the stairs and to the front door in silence. It's the kind of silence that's so big it feels like a whole other person. Taylor never looks at me. She just opens the front door for me and walks away.

I turn around to pull the door closed behind me and hear Taylor say, "Okay buddy, let's go find that dinosaur book. But give me a hug first, okay?" She crouches down, reaches out and gives Zach a hug. Zach doesn't hug her back. He almost never hugs back.

What just happened? I guess I didn't notice Taylor wasn't as excited about being friends with Lacey as I was. And I didn't notice how upset she was when I got to her house today. There's a lot I didn't notice.

I get home earlier than I thought I would and a lot earlier than my mom was expecting me. I go into the kitchen and sit down at the counter. My mom is starting dinner.

"Hi, honey. I thought you'd be at Taylor's house for a while. Is everything okay?"

I thought I didn't want to tell my mom what happened, but I don't know what else to do, so I start talking. I tell her all of it—every terrible part from Lacey's snub, to Madison and Addison's insults, to the fight with Taylor and even the part about my underwear and how I now have *two* horrible nicknames. I don't actually start to cry until I admit that even if I knew what to do, now it's for sure that there's absolutely no way I'll ever be able to get up in front of my class and present my Fifth Farewell. When I finally run out of words, I get ready for what I know is coming. I'm sure my mom is going to have a lot of advice and stories about how hard it is growing up. But she doesn't. She surprises me.

First, she hugs me. Hard. Then she tucks my hair behind my ears. She cups my face with her hands and says, "That is one rotten day. There's only one thing that might help make it better. Ice cream."

"What?" I ask. "Ice cream? Before dinner?" My mom is not a dessert before dinner kind of mom. Ever.

"Yep. Right now. How many scoops?"

My mom gets out two different flavors of ice cream, hot fudge, whipped cream and sprinkles. And we make big, messy, hot fudge sundaes. After I eat mine, I find out my mom was right. I do feel the tiniest bit better. As long as I don't have to leave this kitchen ever again, I think everything might be okay.

word #992

steadfast

able to be trusted or relied on; loyal

"Shut up, Daisy!"

"Annie, don't talk to your little sister like that," my mom says as she walks past my bedroom door.

In our house, no one needs an alarm clock. Daisy wakes up before anyone else. And Daisy wakes up loud. She starts her day with a song—a loud song—and not a song that you'd want to hear first thing in the morning.

But Daisy's serenade is not the reason for my crabby mood this morning. I lie in bed thinking about how much I do not want to get up and go to school today. My stomach is in knots. Do I feel a sore throat coming on, or maybe a fever or something that could convince my mom to let me stay home from school? I swallow twice and then feel my forehead with the back of my hand like my mom always does. Nope. Nothing.

Yesterday was the worst day I ever had. Lacey went over to the dark side. Taylor is totally mad at me. And the entire fifth grade knows that yesterday I was wearing cupcake underwear. What will today be like? I pull the covers up over my head and hide for a while longer.

Once at school, I arrange my folders and pens and then rearrange them while I wait for the morning bell to ring. Well, I'm really waiting for Taylor to arrive—just before the bell, like always. I wanted to call her so many times last night, but I couldn't. I was afraid she might still be mad and not want to talk to me. I can't remember the last time we had a fight.

Jalen walks in, looks right at me and says, "Morning, Cupcake." He cracks up and keeps cracking up, holding onto my desk to keep from falling over with the hilarity of it all. A few of the other kids laugh, too. I don't. I don't say anything either. There's not exactly a right thing to say when someone makes fun of your choice in underwear.

Jalen finally stops laughing and sits down, just in time for me to hear the sound of sneakers slapping down the hall.

Taylor.

Is she still mad at me?

Her locker door slams shut. If Taylor is still mad at me, I'll have to eat lunch alone again today—and maybe for the rest of the year, or maybe even until I graduate high school. I'm guessing that's what happens when your best friend is as mad at you as Taylor was at me yesterday.

The bell rings at the exact second Taylor slides in the door. Instead of going to her desk, she stops in front of mine. I look up at her and notice that her face is a little puffy and swollen. We both say, "I'm so sorry" at exactly the same time. We laugh, which lets me know that we're okay. Before either of us can say anything else, the speaker squawks and Father Richard's voice tells everyone to stand for prayers.

As I make the Sign of the Cross, a giant smile spreads across my face. I'm still upset about Lacey. Yesterday was still a rotten day. And Jalen already called me Cupcake this morning. But my best friend is still my best friend and that makes the rest of it not matter so much.

Taylor and I plop down at the end of our usual cafeteria table with our lunches. I've been dying to talk to her all morning and make sure she knows how sorry I am about yesterday. I think maybe I haven't been a very good friend lately, at least not about the really big stuff. But before I can say anything, Taylor starts talking.

"A chum is someone who's a really close friend, someone you trust with your secrets." She hands me a piece of paper. On it is written one word—*chum*. "When I was trying to find a way to say I was sorry for blowing up at you yesterday, I went looking for different words that meant 'friend.' This was my favorite. It sounds like the kind of friend you would have forever—a best friend," Taylor says. "Like you."

I hold the paper in my hand. Just looking at the word written in Taylor's big, loopy handwriting makes me feel stronger, like nothing Lacey or Madison or even Jalen says can actually touch me. "That's a perfect word—I love it! And I'm sorry, too. I should have noticed that you were upset," I say. "You were right. Your day was a lot worse than mine. I'm really sorry about your mom and everything."

"It's okay. You didn't know. I decided I'm not thinking about my mom today. Yesterday was tragic all around." She rolls her eyes and laughs. But just for a minute. Because here's that look again. The one that means she's not going to tell me what she's thinking or how she's feeling. I hate that look. And it seems like it's kind of the opposite of what she just said about trusting me with all her secrets.

I ignore the thought that's trying to work its way from the back of my brain to the front, the part about keeping my word collection—and what I might do with it—secret from Taylor.

Taylor looks around and then leans forward and says, "I never liked Lacey as much as you did, but this clone thing is weird. I can't believe she got sucked in by them." We look over at the next table where Addison, Madison and Lacey sit whispering and giggling. Great, they're probably planning their next attack.

"It's bizarre. I thought she was nice. Obviously, I was wrong. Or maybe she just didn't like me. Is there something wrong with me? Am I that boring?" I'm only half-kidding.

"What? No. You can't think that. Whatever Lacey's problem is, it's Lacey's problem. And it's a big one. She never talked about anything but how she wished she wasn't here. I don't know why she did what she did, but it's not because of you," says Taylor.

"I know." But I don't. Not really. "Anyway, I hate that I'm worrying about every little thing I told her or talked to her about. If she tells Madison and Addison, they'll have new ammunition for making fun of me."

"At least you didn't tell her you like Sam," says Taylor. "Or did you?"

I almost spit out my sandwich. "What are you talking about?" I've never said anything to Taylor—or anyone else—about my weird feelings. I stare down at my lunch. I don't want to see what she's thinking.

"I can tell. Last week when he asked me about science homework after school, you stood there staring at him with a moony look on your face. And when he said something to you, your cheeks turned pink," says Taylor. I get up the nerve to look at her and she's not laughing or looking like she's making fun of me. "It's okay if you have a crush on Sam. I don't get it. I don't get having a crush on any boy in our class, but it's okay."

"I know, but I hate it," I say. "I don't want to like him. But the other day, I was staring at his freckles in class and thinking how cute they were." I put my head down on the table. "I can't believe I just told you that."

"I can't believe you just told me that either," says Taylor. When I look up, she's smiling but not laughing. "I promise not to make fun of you. And I won't say anything to anyone."

Taylor sits and thinks for a minute. "I can't believe you like boys."

"It's 'boy.' I like *one* boy. And it's a maybe. I'm not sure if that's what it is. I just get a weird feeling around him. I hope it goes away soon," I say.

I'm propped up in bed reading—only three chapters to go in what might be my new favorite book for this year (it depends on how it ends)—when there's a tap on my bedroom door. It's a mom tap. I can tell. My dad is more of a banger.

"Come in." I keep my finger in the exact spot I left off and hope whatever my mom wants, it's fast.

She comes all the way in and closes the door behind her before sitting on the end of my bed. So, probably not fast.

"Did you know I never learned how to ride a bike?" she asks.

"What?"

"A bike. I don't know how to ride a bike." My mom's cheeks turn pink and she starts smoothing my quilt over and over.

"But everyone knows how to ride a bike," I say. "Didn't Grandma or Grandpa teach you?"

"Grandpa tried. But the first time he took off my training wheels, I got going way too fast—our house was at the top of a slope—and I crashed . . . into a tree." More quilt smoothing and not looking up.

"Um, did you get hurt?"

"Yes." My mom finally looks at me and smiles just a bit. "Well, not the kind of hurt where I ended up with a cast or stitches or anything, but the kind where there were a lot of band-aids."

"But didn't you try again?" I ask.

"Nope." Now my mom looks me full in the face. "I was too afraid it would happen again."

"Oh."

"But you know what? I watched all my friends and my brother and sister ride all over the neighborhood. They always looked like they were having so much fun."

I don't know what to say. Because I don't think my mom's just talking about riding a bike. Somehow this is about me and Puddles and my Fifth Farewell.

"I'll let you get back to your book. Lights out in twenty minutes, okay?"

I nod.

My mom kisses me on the top of my head and leaves.

word #993

ambush

a sudden and unexpected attack from a concealed position

Right after the morning bell, Mr. Summer sits on the edge of his desk to talk to us—but not about math. "It's been a great year and I'm proud of each of you. I'm going to miss you. But, we have some things planned for next week that I hope will give each of you a great send off." Mr. Summer likes talking about feelings and he talks a lot about making memories, kinda like my mom. I don't have any proof, but I suspect he's also a scrapbooker.

"So, next week we'll be participating in field day with the rest of the school," Mr. Summer says.

Oh great, field day. It's like torture. We have to play a bunch of games like balloon toss, three-legged race, dodge ball and kickball. For those of

us who are not jocks or tomboys or even especially coordinated, it's not half as much fun as the
teachers think it is.

"We'll also have our Fifth Farewell project presentations so don't forget to sign up for your slot,"
he says.

Hmm. Maybe if I just don't sign up, then I
won't have to stand up in front of the class and
faint, or throw up, or worse. It could work. I wonder if Mr. Summer will notice.

"I have a surprise for all of you. I had some
parents come to me and ask if they could plan a
class party, a dance actually." Mr. Summer looks
kind of confused or maybe surprised.

Groans come from every boy in the room.
Trevor says, "Why would we want a dance? Do we
have to go?"

"Yes, Trevor. We'll all be going. It's a class celebration. You'll have a good time," says Mr.
Summer. More groans. "There will be snacks."
Now there's some laughter. "Two of our class
moms have been nice enough to plan this for all
of you. So, let's remember to thank Mrs. Marinelli
and Mrs. Kim."

Mrs. Marinelli and Mrs. Kim are Madison and
Addison's moms. This dance cannot be a good
thing. Taylor stretches her leg across the aisle and
kicks mine. She agrees.

The rest of the morning is like any other day: hand in homework, take notes, ace a vocabulary quiz. Meaning there's nothing interesting enough to keep questions from bouncing around in my brain. Why are we having a dance? Will anyone ask me to dance? Do I want anyone to ask me to dance? Will Sam ask me to dance?

Taylor and I rush through lunch and head for a quiet spot on the playground, far enough away from everyone else to not be overheard. Jenna and Abby are right behind us.

"Hey, do you guys know anything about this dance?" asks Abby. "I thought dances didn't start until middle school. And that's not until next year." Abby looks like she's inches away from total panic.

"What I want to know is why Madison and Addison's moms are planning it and what does that *mean*?" says Taylor.

"Taylor's right. That's the part that's worrying me," I say. "Is this a big plan to do something awful to us? Or is this just part of Madison and Addison being all into boys now? They're always whispering and pointing at Sam and Jack and Trevor and hanging around them."

Jenna chews on her lip and twirls a chunk of her hair—the same things she does when she's working on a so-hard-only-she-can-figure-it-out math problem. Taylor just shrugs.

"Um, do you guys want to dance with anyone?" Abby asks. From the way she's trying to be casual about it, it's obvious *she* does.

I sneak a glance at Taylor. She is purposely not looking at me. My secret is safe.

Taylor says, "I don't want to dance with anyone. And I can't believe that any of the boys want to dance with any of the girls, especially not Madison or Addison."

"None of the boys will dance with me because I'm taller than all of them," says Abby. She's the tallest kid in our class. "What if everyone gets asked to dance except me?"

"Let's not worry about it. We'll go, have cake and dance together to the fast songs. If they play slow songs, we head for the snack table," says Taylor. She sounds so sure.

"That's a good plan. I like it," says Jenna.

I don't say anything. I don't know how I feel. Will Sam ask me to dance? If he does, what am I supposed to say? Do I even want him to ask me to dance? Will someone else ask me? Just thinking about it makes me feel sick to my stomach.

"Oh girls, you look so serious. What are you talking about?"

We were so into our conversation about the dance that we didn't notice Madison and Addison—with Lacey trailing behind—coming our way, snotty looks in place as usual.

"Do not worry about it Addison. Or is it Madison? Or now Lacey? It's so hard to tell you girls apart these days. But I guess it doesn't matter—you all share a brain anyway," says Taylor.

Wow! Taylor always says she's not afraid of them, but she's never said anything like that before.

Madison and Addison look at each other and kind of sputter for a minute. Lacey looks right at Taylor, opens her mouth like she's going to say something, and then just closes it and looks at the ground.

Madison recovers first. "Like we care what you think, Taylor," she says. "I just hope you girls don't think any of the boys will ask you to dance. What boy would look at any of you when they could dance with us? Annie is too skinny and boring. Taylor is just a mess with a mouth full of metal. Jenna's brain is too big and Abby is too tall." And with that, Madison nods at her little fan club like she's pleased with herself and they all walk away.

Abby kind of slouches to try to make herself look shorter and Jenna's eyes are shiny with tears. I turn to Taylor and say, "Whoa, why'd you do that?"

"Yeah, why'd you make them so mad, Taylor? It only makes them meaner." Abby sounds like she might cry, too.

"Don't worry about what they said. None of it's true anyway," says Taylor. "I'm tired of them walking around being horrible to everyone and getting away with it. I'm sorry they were mean to you, but I'm not sorry I said it."

"I guess I'm not sorry you said it either," I say. "The looks on their faces were pretty funny. Lacey kept opening and closing her mouth like a fish." I giggle and make my best fish face.

"You're right. It was funny. They didn't know what to say," says Jenna. She starts to laugh, too. After a minute, Abby joins in.

We're all cracking up about how Taylor put Addison, Madison and Lacey in their places when I look over at them. They are looking back. Message received.

This is so not over.

word #994

haven

a place of safety, shelter, or comfort

After school, I collapse on my too pink bed and think about what to think about first. Not the dance. I can't—there's too much about it that's freaking me out. Instead, I decide to start with the thing that's freaking me out just a little bit less than the dance—my self-portrait project.

The problem is that it's too loud at my house this afternoon to think about anything at all. Daisy has two of her friends over to play and, like Daisy, they are not quiet. They're playing a game where they sing songs at the top of their lungs while twirling in circles. The winner is the last one to fall down. It's a fun game to play when you're seven—and even sometimes when you're eleven. But it's not a quiet game. And it's not good for thinking.

I run down the stairs and, as I open the front door, yell, "Mom, I'm going to the library."

"Be careful and be home in time to set the table for dinner," she says.

No problem. An hour should do it. I grab my notebook and go.

My feet know the way. Go down the street fourteen houses. Turn right at the corner. Go four more houses. Cross the street and I'm there. I walk in, take a deep breath and inhale the aroma of thousands of books and millions of words. Taylor complains it smells musty like her great grandmother's house, but I love it. I've been coming here as long as I can remember—first, for story time with my mom when I was little, and now on my own.

"Annie! How are you?" Mrs. Richardson is the children's librarian and she knows everything about every book here.

"Hi, Mrs. Richardson. Any new books?"

She always saves new books for me that she thinks I'll like.

"We're getting one later this week that I'll set aside for you. I read it and I know you'll love it." Mrs. Richardson gives me a big smile.

"Sounds great! I'll come by again on Saturday and see you. I've got a school project to work on today." I wave to her and head back to my spot.

Next to my bench in the backyard, this is my favorite spot to sit and read, or think. It's a little nook in the back of the kids' section that you can't see easily. You have to know it's there. There's a perfectly comfortable red corduroy chair that's soft and cozy from being sat in for years and years. It's worn and in some spots the ridges have been rubbed so smooth that it isn't really corduroy anymore. Still, when I snuggle down in it just right, it feels like a hug. And the window looks out at a patch of grass and a birch tree. Birch trees are my favorite; I love the curly pieces of bark on their trunks. The leaves are still new and greener than green.

Perfect.

I used to think this spot had magical powers. Maybe it still does. I just hope any magic it does have works on me today. My presentation is next week and the only thing I know for sure is that I don't know anything for sure. I wrote out a character profile like I'd do for a book report. It's okay, but it doesn't feel right. Then there's my word collection. How can I use it? Do I want to use it?

Looking for help, I open my word collection notebook to the first page. *Onomatopoeia.* That was the word that got me started. It was the first word I ever collected and a category of words in my collection. There are so many things to love about the word *onomatopoeia*. It's completely fun to say. And, even better, words that are onomatopoeias are *also* fun to say. They're words that sound like what they mean like *slurp, squish, thud, vroom,* and *fizz* (which are all words in my collection).

My words tell a lot about me. They say that I'm funnier than you might think. I've collected funny sounding words like *gobbledygook, kibitz, hubbub* and *geezer.* I love the word *geezer.* Not just any old man can be a *geezer.* Then there are the words that mean different laughs like *chortle, chuckle, giggle* and *guffaw.* I even collected the word *flatulence* (the boys in my class would like that one) which means the same thing as fart. And some of my words, like *nincompoop* and *akimbo* (which means standing with your hands on your hips and your elbows out to your sides) are just plain fun to say.

My words also say that I'm creative. Not the drawing or painting or craft kind of creative like Taylor or Daisy or even my mom with her scrapbooks, but creative with words and ideas.

I collect words that describe how I feel about things . . . good things and sometimes not so good things. I like to find exactly the right word to describe a feeling. Happy feelings like ecstatic, gleeful, blissful or joyous, and sad feelings like angst, melancholy or forlorn. Each one means a different kind of happy or sad. And when I'm nervous about something, if I can figure out what word best describes just what kind of nervous it is, it helps me calm down. Like, am I just apprehensive? Or is it really bad and I'm petrified? Thinking of the perfect word to describe the feeling I'm feeling helps me make sense of it.

How I feel right now is frustrated . . . and flummoxed. I have all these words, almost 1,000. Words I can use to describe anything and anyone. But are they the right words to describe me? To truly make a picture of me?

I hear Mrs. Richardson say hi to someone and that someone answers her. Yikes! It's Sam. He's never gotten the hang of the whole quiet-in-the-library thing. What is Sam doing here? He doesn't come to the library anymore.

Sam's head pops around the corner and he smiles at me. "Hey Annie! I knew this was where you'd be," he says.

"How'd you know?" I ask. And "why were you looking" is what I don't ask.

"You showed me this spot when we used to come here with our moms, remember? When

Mrs. Richardson said you were in the library, I knew you'd be here," Sam says.

"Logical," I say, half to myself. Which is another way of saying boring.

"So, what's up?" I ask. I try hard to act casual. I tell myself that my face is hot because it's warm in here and I clutch my notebook so my hands won't shake. But I'm with Sam in a space that's really only big enough for one person. Again, yikes.

"Well, I came to get a book to help me with my project and when Mrs. Richardson told me you were here, I wanted to ask how yours is going," says Sam.

"I'm not sure," I say. "I can't seem to decide what I want to do."

"Hey, it's your notebook!" I forgot I was still holding it. I try to shove it behind my back, but it's too late. He's already seen. "Do you still collect words? Are you going to use your word collection?" he asks. I look up at him to see if he's making fun of me like Madison and Addison did. He's not.

"Maybe. I'm not sure," I say. "What are you doing for yours?"

"Well, I think I'm going to make a baseball card of myself," says Sam. "That's why I needed this book—it has a bunch of old baseball cards in it. I know everybody probably thinks I'll do something funny or get up and make jokes, but baseball is what I really care about." Sam shifts from one foot to the other and looks out the window. "Do you think that's a dumb idea?"

"No, not dumb at all. I think it's a good idea. It's a picture, which is what the assignment is, and it's something that matters to you. I think that's what Mr. Summer wants us to do."

"Well, thanks. Now I have to figure out how to put it all together." Sam looks at his watch. "Hey, it's almost five-thirty. I have to get home. Are you ready to leave yet? I'll walk with you."

Okay, I need to be cool about this. It's Sam—we live across the street from each other and I've known him as long as I can remember. Yes, he has cute freckles and floppy hair. But, it's just Sam. Relax.

"Sure, I need to get home anyway to set the table," I say.

"Humphrey family dinnertime is still six o'clock?" Sam grins.

I smile back. "You know my mom loves a good schedule," I say. "Let's go."

I put my notebook in my backpack and we leave the library. "Goodbye you two," says Mrs. Richardson. She's smiling at us the way adults do when they think you're cute. I pretend not to notice.

"So Annie, I think it'd be cool to use your word collection, but I don't get how it would work. Words aren't pictures. I thought we had to use a picture."

"Well, you know the saying about a picture being worth a thousand words?" I ask.

"Yeah, I guess."

"Well, I'm getting close to having one thousand words in my collection. And I got to thinking that my words can be my picture. Words can make a picture." I don't know if Sam is getting what I'm trying to say. I sneak a look at his face and can see from his wrinkled forehead that nope, he's not so I try again.

"Like, you know how when you're reading a book, you get pictures in your mind about the story?" Still nothing. "Okay, how about this? If I tell you about a baseball game I saw, and I tell you how the shadows cut across the infield, and how the dirt and dust got kicked up when the batter tapped the bat against his cleats, and how one of the players slid into third base and barely beat the tag, can you start to see a picture of it in your mind?" Somehow, it's important to me to make Sam understand.

"Yeah, I can. That's cool. You know I don't read much anymore, so I guess I'm out of practice. But yeah, I can almost see that guy sliding into third. Awesome," says Sam. He looks at me and smiles.

We're on the sidewalk in front of my house.

"Have a fun Humphrey family dinner. See you later," says Sam.

"Yeah, see you tomorrow." I shrug and wave.

Sam runs across the street, jumps over his mom's flower border and goes inside. Sigh. I turn and shuffle up the walk to my own front door.

word #995

neophyte

a beginner or novice at any activity

My body walks in the front door of my house, but my mind is still back on the sidewalk with Sam. I hoped Sam would get what my words mean to me. I don't think he did. Maybe nobody else will either.

"Annie, is that you?" yells my mom from the kitchen. "I need you to set the table. Dinner is in five minutes."

Daydreaming over, I head into the kitchen. My mom is finishing up dinner and Daisy is working on her homework at the counter. The frown that looks so out of place on her face says it's not going well.

"Hi, Mom. Hey, Daisy. What are you working on?" I arrange four placemats and four napkins on the table.

"I have a spelling test tomorrow. Mommy was quizzing me and I got almost all of them wrong." She looks up at me and says, "I'm not good at spelling like you are. It's not fair." Her lower lip quivers, a sure sign Daisy is going to cry.

"Don't worry, I can help you after dinner," I say.

"Okay," she says and sniffles. "Thanks, I guess."

My mom and I smile at each other and she whispers, "Thank you." I finish pouring water for everyone just as my dad comes in, and we sit down to eat.

"Annie, your mom told me there's some kind of fifth grade dance next week," says my dad. "I don't think I like the idea of you going to a dance." Sometimes, like now, my dad acts like I'm still Daisy's age.

"Dances are usually only for the middle school." I shrug. "It's not a big deal. We'll have some snacks and cake and they'll play music. That's all." I try hard to sound casual. I think it's working. I hope it's working. The last thing I want is to have a big "conversation" about this. "Brian, don't worry about it," says my mom. "I'm going to chaperone so I'll make sure everything is fine." And there's the smile my mom smiles when she wants me to think something is a great idea when it's obvious that it's exactly the opposite of a great idea.

"What?" I ask. "You're going to chaperone? Are you serious?" And just like that, my Fifth Farewell presentation is *not* my biggest worry. For right now, anyway. Because the last thing any kid wants at her first dance is her mom watching from behind the punchbowl.

"Well, if Mom is going to be there, I guess it's okay," says my dad.

Oh yeah, I'm sure that will make things so much better. But I don't say that. I don't say anything. The taco that was so delicious a minute ago now tastes like cardboard. This is what dread tastes like.

"A dance? How fun!" says Daisy. "I love to dance. I wish I could go. I would wear one of my fancy dresses. What are you going to wear?"

What am I going to wear? I hadn't thought of that. One of the good things about wearing a uniform to school is not having to think about what I wear. One of the bad things is that I don't know or care much about fashion.

"Um, I don't know. I guess just a pair of jeans and a T-shirt," I say. Daisy gives me a look of disgust that I don't think I should be getting from my little sister. "You can't wear a T-shirt," she says. "It's a dance. You have to look special. Mom, tell her!" Well, at least this got her mind off of the spelling test.

"Daisy's right, honey," says my mom. "You know, it would be fun for you to get a new outfit. Other than your school uniform and a couple outfits for church, all of your clothes are so casual. Let's go shopping Saturday."

"I don't know, Mom. Can't I just wear something I already have? You know I don't like shopping." I'm missing that thing that makes most girls, including Daisy and my mom, love to shop for clothes.

"How about if you see if Taylor wants to come, too?" my mom asks. "We could have lunch out and make a day of it. Dad can take Daisy to dance class and spend the day with her."

"Okay, that might be fun. I'll call Taylor after dinner and ask her," I say. If Taylor comes, it might be bearable.

"Well, if you're going to a dance, you'll need to know how to dance," says my dad. "How about if I show you some steps after dinner?"

Well, that sounds embarrassing, but my dad looks so earnest. I don't want to do this, but I don't want to hurt his feelings either.

"Okay, Dad. Just for a couple of minutes, though. I have homework."

After dinner, my dad turns the stereo to some station that plays what he calls "easy listening." I call it, songs you hear while riding in an elevator.

"Okay, put this hand here on my shoulder and then the other hand in mine." My dad gets me into what I guess is the right position. "Now just follow my lead."

The next thing my dad says is, "Ow! Okay, that was my foot. Maybe we need to start again."

"I'm sorry. I don't know how to follow your lead. I don't even know what that means," I say. "Let's just forget it."

"No way. We're not giving up yet. Let's try this," says my dad. "Take your left foot and step forward, then have your right foot follow it. Then slide to the right with your right foot and then follow that with your left. Got it?"

"Uh, no. Not at all. But let's try one more time," I say. All I want is to get this over with. Fast.

This time isn't quite as bad. I manage to get through a couple of steps before Daisy says, "Who do you think is gonna ask you to dance, Annie?"

Whoops—I just stepped on my dad's foot again—harder this time.

"I'm sorry, Dad. It was an accident," I say. He kind of smiles at me but he's wincing, too. "I don't want to dance with anyone. I don't want anyone to ask me to dance. This is silly, I'm going to do my homework," I say and stalk out of the living room.

As I climb the stairs, and trip on the fourth one, I look back to see Daisy dancing expertly with my dad. It doesn't look like she needs my help with anything.

word #996

mettle

boldness, strength of character

As I pull my favorite pale blue T-shirt over my head there's a fast, and loud, banging on my door. Only one person announces herself that way. Before I can tell her to come in, the door bursts open and there's Taylor, beaming. That is, beaming with something stuck in her braces.

"Hey! Are you ready? Your mom said to tell you she wants to leave in ten minutes." The plate Taylor is carrying has two blueberry muffins on it—one with a huge bite out of it. Mystery solved—the something that's stuck in her braces is a blueberry. "She sent these with me. They're still warm. Mmmm. I love your mom."

"Yum. Yes, I'm ready to go. Give me my muffin before you eat both of them," I say. "What's in the bag?" Taylor has a huge tote bag slung over her shoulder.

"I finished my Fifth Farewell project last night and I want to show it to you," says Taylor. "I'm kind of excited about it."

"Let me see," I say. I feel a twinge knowing that Taylor is done with her project when I'm not.

Taylor unzips her backpack and pulls out something totally unexpected. It's the size and shape of the globe that sits on a stand in our classroom. But everything else about it is like nothing I've ever seen. It's painted bright orange and yellow and is covered with photographs and pictures cut out from magazines.

"Wow! I think I love it," I say. "What is it?"

"What do you mean what is it? It's me!" says Taylor. "See, I started trying to do something on a piece of poster board. But it was too flat. So then I thought about how there's more than one side to me and how there are a lot of different things that are important to me. So, I thought I'd do something different. Check it out, it's an *orb*." Taylor laughs.

She's laughing at me. Taylor loves to use my words on me. I once collected the word *orb*, which means a sphere or a globe, mostly because I liked how it sounded. For some reason, Taylor thinks it's hilarious. She looks for opportunities to say it, which thankfully are not easy to find.

I swat Taylor with my shoe and then put it on. "Okay, you're not as funny as you think you are," I say. Actually, she is. "Now tell me about your orb."

"Well, there are pictures that show all the different things I am. You know, daughter, best friend—see this one of us, student and big sister." Taylor runs her finger over a picture of her with Zach and is quiet for a minute. I stay quiet, too. She has a small, soft smile on her face that I think of as her Zach smile. It's a smile but somehow it looks sad.

After a minute, Taylor looks up at me. She says, "Can I ask you something?"

"Anything," I say.

Taylor turns her project around and around in her hands. She doesn't look up when she says, "Last week my mom made us go see a family counselor. He asked me how I feel about Zach's autism. I said I didn't know. Then he asked if I was ever embarrassed by or ashamed of Zach. I tried to say no but then I couldn't . . . because it wasn't true." Taylor looks right at me. I've never seen anyone look so sad. "Does that make me a horrible person?"

"No," I say as fast as I can. "No, you're not a horrible person."

Taylor finally wants to talk about Zach. I can't mess this up. I say, "This is a big thing. A huge thing. And you're a great big sister. I promise."

"Thanks," says Taylor. "That's kind of what the counselor said. And he said there's no right way to feel. But I'm not sure my mom agrees with him."

Taylor gives her head a quick shake and says, "Okay, back to my *orb*. I also have pictures of all kinds of stuff that I love. See, I went through a bunch of magazines and found pictures of pizza, cookies, flowers, cupcakes, and music."

"Wow." I mean it this time. "It's perfect." It is. It's one-of-a-kind and creative and perfectly Taylor. "I think it'll be different from what anyone else does—in a good way."

"Yay!" Taylor says and does a little dance. "I like it, but I wanted to make sure it wasn't too crazy."

"It is crazy, but not too crazy." I smile. "Just like you."

Taylor makes what she thinks is a crazy face at me. And now she has three blueberries stuck in her braces.

"Girls, let's go," my mom yells up the stairs. "I'll be waiting out in the van."

I sigh in dramatic fashion. I read that in a book once and try to do it when it fits the situation. It fits this situation: shopping.

"Okay, let's get this over with," I say. Taylor and I run down the stairs and out the front door. "Oh and by the way, you have blueberries stuck in your braces," I say back over my shoulder.

The drive to the mall takes forever. When we finally get there, we park close to the Italian restaurant that makes the best pizza in the world. As she opens her door, my mom says, "I thought the promise of a pizza lunch might make shopping a little less painful. Was I right?" She's smiling. She knows she's right.

"Yes, Mom. That might help a little," I say. What I don't tell her is that if she throws in some ice cream for dessert, I might even have fun.

"A little? Are you crazy? Do you remember their pizza? Can we just skip shopping and go now?" asks Taylor. She's not kidding.

"Nope. Come on girls, fashion before food." My mom leads the way into the mall.

"I'm sure we'll be able to find something darling for both of you girls here," my mom says.

I don't know what something "darling" looks like but I'm sure it's not something I want to wear.

"Now, have you thought about if you want to wear a dress or a skirt?" she asks.

"No. But why are pants not one of my choices?" I ask. Ever since the whole cupcake underpants incident, I like wearing skirts even less. I've been wearing a pair of gym shorts under my school uniform skirt. I don't care if it makes me look a little lumpy. Better lumpy than humiliated.

"Oh, Annie. It's your first dance. Will you at least try on some skirts and dresses?" asks my mom. "This section looks cute. Why don't you girls look through these racks and pick a few things to try on."

"Okay, fine. We'll look. Come on Taylor. Do you know what you're looking for?" I ask her.

"Not really," she says. "Something different—something a little loud, maybe. You know, like me." And she pulls out a couple of dresses and a skirt in some of the brightest colors I've ever seen.

"Well, no chance we'll pick the same outfit." I grin at Taylor. "I guess this dress and this skirt aren't so bad. Maybe I could wear the skirt with a white T-shirt or tank."

"Gee Annie, don't go too crazy," says Taylor.

Just what I don't need from her right now: sarcasm. I look at what I picked. I guess they are a little boring. "Fine, I'll try harder." I pick out a few things that don't look like me and we head for the dressing rooms.

Taylor and I try on outfits and twirl around in front of the three-way mirror. My mom laughs and gives her opinions about each outfit. It's almost fun. Then, in the middle of a twirl, I jerk to a stop. Oh, no. In the mirror I see Madison Marinelli's mother striding our way. Madison trails after her, snotty look firmly in place.

Before I have a chance to warn Taylor or my mom, they're upon us.

"Oh, Callie. How nice to see you," Mrs. Marinelli says to my mom. She smiles, sort of. It's the kind of smile that doesn't reach her eyes—a fake smile. What my mom calls "insincere." My mom hates insincere.

"Mimi. Oh, and Madison. Well, it has been a while," says my mom. Yikes. There's the pressed-lip look again.

I look at Taylor in the mirror. She whispers, "The incident." I try, unsuccessfully, not to laugh. Now the pressed-lip look comes my way. Oops.

I haven't seen Mrs. Marinelli since my mom left the parent organization. It happened right around the time Mr. Marinelli got a big job and their family moved to the biggest house in town.

"Are you and Annie shopping for something for the dance?" asks Mrs. Marinelli. "Madison and all of her friends are so excited. She deserves a special celebration for graduating from fifth grade and, since the school didn't seem to be planning anything, I took care of it."

Madison stands next to her mother with her arms crossed over her chest and rolls her eyes. It's impossible to tell if she's directing her unpleasantness at her mother or at us. Probably both. But what does her mom mean "all of her friends"? Madison has always had exactly one friend. Addison. Then I remember Lacey. I guess Madison has two friends now. Still, two isn't all of anything, especially not friends.

"Yes, well. I'm here with Annie and Taylor. We're having a fun day together," says my mom. She has a funny look on her face. My mom is a very friendly person and has a great smile. She's not smiling now. In fact, she looks like she just noticed an unpleasant smell.

Madison has been standing next to her mother looking Taylor and me up and down. Finally, she speaks. "Oh, yes. I can see that you're trying a new look, Taylor. Interesting." The way she says it leaves no doubt that she doesn't mean interesting in a good way. "And Annie, I can see that you're not trying anything new. That dress is perfect for you—perfectly ordinary."

Shopping is bad. Shopping while Madison Marinelli watches is worse. But what she says next is *the* worst.

"My mom's letting Addison and me plan pretty much the whole dance. Get ready to be surprised." Before Taylor or I have a chance to say anything or to try to figure out what she means by that, Madison walks away to look through the racks of clothes.

"Make sure you find something really cute, Madison," says Mrs. Marinelli loud enough for anyone walking by to hear. "And don't worry about the price tags. Daddy said nothing's too much for his little girl."

Ugh. Seriously?

I can't look at Taylor or I will laugh. Taylor can't, or doesn't try to, keep her snickering quiet. Mrs. Marinelli doesn't seem to notice.

"Michael and I are so proud of her," Mrs. Marinelli tells my mom. "I'm treating her to a whole day of pampering. We're going to get our nails done after this—fingers *and* toes, of course— and then Madison is getting her hair done. You know," she continues, "it's a shame that your Annie and her little friend can't seem to get along with Madison and her friends. I just wish that Annie wasn't so mean to Madison. It's uncalled for. I tell Madison it's just jealousy, that it must be hard for the other girls when Madison is so much prettier and has so much going for her." Mrs. Marinelli opens her mouth to keep talking. The thing she doesn't know is that she has underestimated my mother.

"Well, Mimi that's certainly an interesting version of the truth. I'm sure that is what Madison tells you. It's not the version that I've been told, and not just by my own daughter. Brian and I are proud of Annie for who she is, for her character and honesty and kindness. And we're proud of her for being a good friend, and for choosing her friends based on who they are, not what they have." My mom says all of it without taking a breath.

If you don't know my mother well, nothing about her face gives away just how angry she is. But I know where to look. Her jaw is tight, her neck has small red splotches on it and you can see a vein in her temple bulging. Not since the time I snooped and looked at some of my Christmas presents early have I seen that vein. And I try not to think about that afternoon. Let's just say that some of the presents I saw when I snooped never made it under the Christmas tree.

"Annie and Taylor, why don't you get changed and we'll go for lunch now. I'd really like to wash away the taste of this conversation." And without saying another word, my mom makes it perfectly clear to Mrs. Marinelli that the conversation is over.

Taylor and I hurry back to the dressing room to change back into our own clothes.

"Whoa, that was unbelievable," says Taylor. "I didn't know your mom had it in her."

"Me either."

word #997

audacious

very *bold* or adventurous; daring

I breathe deeply and smell *the smell*—grass that's just been cut. For me, that smell means it's almost summer vacation. Here in Michigan, by the end of summer, the grass will have burnt under the heat of the sun and it doesn't smell like anything. But right now, with June just beginning, it's so green it doesn't look real. My dad finishes mowing our lawn and heads over to where I sit on my bench leaning back against the rough bark of the tree, and munching on a cookie. He hands me one of the two bottles of water he's carrying and plops down next to me.

"Do you smell that? I love that smell," says my dad. He knows I love that smell. We both inhale deeply and loudly. The loudly part makes us laugh. I love my dad's laugh. It isn't loud, but you can almost feel it. It comes from deep within his chest and it makes his shoulders shake. It's one of my favorite sounds.

"Mom told me about her conversation with Mrs. Marinelli at the mall yesterday," says my dad. "She's worried that you might've been upset by it."

"Upset? No," I say. What I'd been was surprised. Well, more like shocked really. I couldn't believe how she put Madison's mom in her place. I wish I could put Madison in her place like that.

"Mom's really brave," I say.

"She is." My dad looks straight into my eyes. "And so are you."

"Not always."

"Nobody's always brave." My dad grins. "Not even me."

I giggle. My dad is insanely scared of snakes, even tiny ones. When we go to the zoo, he won't even go inside the reptile house. Of course, it's Daisy's favorite. Snakes are her favorite animal, especially the giant ones. And I like to look at the turtles. Dad waits for us outside. He calls it "enjoying some fresh air."

Nobody's always brave.

"Hey, Dad, do you know Mom doesn't know how to ride a bike?"

"Yep. I tried to teach her once. It was when you were just a baby." He makes a nervous face and rubs his knee. "I bought her a new bike for her birthday. It had a bell and even a basket on the handlebars to hold flowers. It didn't go very well."

"Did she fall?"

"Nope. I did." Now he rubs his shoulder. "I was trying to show her how easy it was. I was busy *telling* her how easy it was when I ran smack into Mrs. Patel's mailbox."

"Yikes."

"Yep."

And with that, my dad stands up, kisses me on the top of my head, and heads for the house. The back door opens just before my dad gets there and Taylor pops out. She giggles at something my dad says, comes half skipping over to my bench and flops down next to me.

"Hey! So, your dad tells me you're out here thinking deep thoughts and eating cookies. At least one of those sounds like fun," she says and smiles.

"Hey, yourself. I'm thinking about my project," I say. And about how I'm not brave. And about how even if my presentation is awesome—and it might be—getting up in front of the class and telling everyone about it won't be awesome. It could be tragic . . . and humiliating . . . again.

"So, my presentation is Thursday. Yours is Friday. Mine's done, yours isn't. Do you see what I'm saying?" Taylor asks.

"I know. But, it's kind of done. Well, maybe," I say.

"Kind of? Maybe? Explain, please," says Taylor. "Hey, are there any more cookies?"

"Are we talking about cookies or my presentation?" I ask.

"Sorry. It's just that I could smell them when I walked through the kitchen. Peanut butter, right? Sorry. Okay, start talking."

"Well, I've done more than you think. I have a presentation right now," I say. It's true, sort of. "And here, of course there are more cookies."

"Okay, keep talking," says Taylor. She's chewing with her eyes closed, but I know she's listening—really listening—like only a best friend listens.

"I finally decided that my self-portrait is going to be something I've been working on for a long time: my word collection." Taylor gasps and then smiles and nods. She gets it. "By then I'll have one thousand words. And I'm going to talk about how words can make pictures, and how my words make pictures of me," I say. "But..."

Taylor's eyes snap open, she sits up straight, reaches over and grabs my arm. Hard. "But what? Come on Annie, what are you going to do?"

"I don't know. I mean, do you remember second grade?"

"Yeah, of course I remember second grade. I spent the entire year trying to convince my mom and dad to get me a horse. Instead I got Zach." Taylor rolls her eyes and smiles.

"No, I mean do you remember me in second grade?"

"Uh-huh."

"Do you remember why Madison and Addison started calling me Puddles?"

"Annie, that was a long time ago. And it's not going to happen again."

I chew on my lip and dig at the ground with the toe of my sneaker.

"It's not," Taylor repeats with the confidence that I don't feel.

I shrug.

"Annie, this is important," says Taylor. "At first I couldn't figure out what Mr. Summer wanted from us and then I kept changing my mind about what to do. But once I got started, it was really cool. Putting together something that was just about me was fun." She pops the last of her cookie into her mouth. "I guess I could get made fun of for it, but I don't care."

"You don't. But I do. I mean, yes it's the end of fifth grade. But we're taking all of the same peo-ple into sixth grade with us," I say.

"True. And I thought about that. I don't love it when Madison and Addison tell me I'm a mess or make fun of my hair or my braces, but I don't care what they think anymore," says Taylor.

"I know. And that's what I've been thinking about."

"Tell me about your presentation," says Taylor.

"I don't know if I can," I say.

Taylor looks away and takes a deep breath in through her nose. I know she's getting impatient with me. What she doesn't understand is that it's not easy for me. I talk about being myself—and I am—but quietly. Taylor is Taylor right out loud. She is so sure of herself—my mom calls it her "unwavering confidence." No matter what, Taylor believes in herself. I'm still working on it.

"I'm so over Addison, Madison, and now Lacey having power over the rest of us. So they don't like us. So they say mean things to us. Do you *want* them to like you? Do you *want* to be friends with them? Do *you* like *them*?" Taylor asks.

"No. No. And of course not," I say.

"So don't worry about what they might think. Give your presentation. I think you should go for it," says Taylor.

"Go for it? Me? I don't go for it. That's you," I say.

"What do you mean?"

"Think about it. When we go to the pool, how do I get in the water?" I ask.

There's a pool in the park in our neighborhood and Taylor and I go there most days during the summer. It's where we both learned to swim when we were little. And it's the place where our friendship began the summer before kindergarten. We were both splashing around in the shallow end wearing the same purple floaties when Taylor paddled over and asked me to be her friend.

"You get in inch by inch," says Taylor. She smiles. "It drives me crazy. I have to stop myself from just pushing you in. Hmm, maybe this year . . ." Now her smile changes and it matches the glint in her eyes—trouble.

"Don't ever do that!" I say. I make a mental note to watch Taylor closely the next time we go swimming. "And how do you get in?"

"You know how I get in," she says. "Cannonball into the deep end. It's important to make a big splash."

It's true. For Taylor, getting into the pool is an event.

"Exactly. I'm a toe dipper. I get in slowly, warming up as I go. You jump in all at once and make a lot of noise. That's what I'm saying. You go for it. I don't," I say.

What I don't tell Taylor is that even if I want to go for it, I don't know if I can.

word #998

perspective

the way things are seen from a particular
point of view

I walk out the back door of our school and look
out over the playing fields. Field day. At first it
looks chaotic. There are kids everywhere. But
there's a method to this madness. It's all about
T-shirts.

Each class wears a different color. The first
graders are in sunshine yellow. They trail across
the soccer field in a crooked line on their way to
the potato sack race. I see that part of the reason
the line is crooked is that Daisy is its leader—she
twirls and dances as she goes. The second graders, in electric blue, run around screaming as a
teacher tries to get them organized into teams for
the water balloon toss. Some of the balloons won't
make it to the start of the game. The kickball field

is a sea of red-shirted third graders. The fourth graders, in lime green, pelt each other with dodge balls. And over next to the baseball diamond is my class, in orange. They wait for the start of the three-legged race. I plod over to join them.

"Now that everyone is here, I'll put you in teams." Mrs. Storkmeyer gives instructions as I walk up and stand at the edge of the group. Our fourth grade teacher is in charge of the three-legged race.

"Let's see. For our first group, how about Sam and Oliver, Madison and Abby, Taylor and Jenna, Jalen and Trevor, Alex and Addison, and . . . ," she says. I stop listening. I've already figured out that the only other person left in our group is Lacey. I have to do the three-legged race with Lacey. Lacey, who hasn't said one word to me since before Taylor's birthday party . . .

I take the white scarf that we'll use to tie our legs together from Mrs. Storkmeyer and, for a minute, I'm not sure what to do. I feel nervous, but decide to just act like it's not a big deal. I walk over to where Lacey stands staring at the ground and twirling a piece of her hair.

"Let's tie this on and get this over with," I say.

"Okay," says Lacey.

And now we're tied together. Silence.

We wait for Mrs. Storkmeyer to start the race. We start to run and within a few steps, we fall behind. And then fall down. I untie our legs and get up, still saying nothing. The teams that are still running are those that look like they have a strategy. They have their arms around each other's shoulders and are talking to each other as they run. Go figure.

I decide to walk to the finish line to meet up with Taylor and Jenna. They came in second behind Jalen and Trevor. I've taken a couple steps when Lacey finally says something.

"Annie?"

I stop. I don't say anything, but I do turn around and look at her. Lacey's chewing on her lip and playing with her hair. I raise my eyebrows into a question without words.

"Can I tell you something?" Lacey asks. She doesn't wait for me to answer. "It's just that, well I'm really, really sorry. I was so mad at my mom and I found out that my dad isn't coming. Ever. My parents are getting divorced. They didn't even talk to me before they decided. And I was so mad. And I don't know why I did what I did. It didn't help anything. It just made everything worse." Her voice is shaking. But before she can say anything else, Madison comes over, grabs Lacey by the arm, and drags her away while glaring at me.

What was that? So Lacey's sorry. And her parents are getting a divorce, which is awful. Other than that, I have no idea what she was trying to tell me. But it sounds like she wishes she hadn't signed up to be part of Madison, Addison, and Lacey. I'm not sure if I feel bad for her, or if I'm still mad, or both.

Taylor waves me over. She has a plan called, *Skip the Start of the Kickball Game and Hide Out behind the Bleachers.* We flop on the grass and look up at the clouds. The sky is as blue as it gets with a few big, puffy clouds of whitest white. It's perfect for cloud watching.

"There was a lot of weirdness in that three-legged race," says Taylor. "Did Lacey say anything to you?"

"Not really." I decide to keep Lacey's news about her parents confidential. "She started to say something, but then Madison came and dragged her off."

"Hmmm. I wonder what she was going to say," says Taylor. "Oh, who cares?"

"Yeah, who cares," I say. But what I don't tell Taylor is that I do care. It still bothers me that Lacey did what she did.

Thunk. In the middle of staring at the biggest cloud in the sky and trying to decide whether it looks more like an elephant or a monkey riding a bike, thunk. Something hits the ground right between our heads. Taylor yelps and I sit up so fast I get dizzy.

A kickball. It's a kickball. Again.

"I'll get it! Hold on!" a voice yells. No way. It's Sam . . . again.

Sam comes flying around the bleachers. "Hey! What are you guys doing here? Wait. Annie, did the ball hit you again? Please say it didn't." He grabs the ball and passes it from one hand to the other.

"No, it didn't hit *us*," says Taylor. "Thanks for caring, Sam."

"Oh good. But hey, what are you guys doing back here?" asks Sam. "Why aren't you in the game?"

"We're just taking a break from field day," I say. "I guess our break is over now."

"Yeah, come on. The game already started. Annie you can be on my team," says Sam as he runs off ahead of us.

Taylor looks at me. Her eyes are in danger of bugging out of her head.

"Okay. Let's go. Annie can be on Sam's team," she says.

And we walk, not run, to join the game.

When field day ends, I actually have a first place ribbon. Somehow, Oliver and I tied for first place in the potato sack race when we both fell over the finish line laughing. And Sam picked me for his team in kickball. Maybe field day isn't so bad after all.

word #999

illuminate

to make clear or easier to understand; explain

As Sam stands at the front of the class giving his presentation, all I can think about is if he'll ask me to dance later today. Today's the day of our fifth grade dance. I wish I didn't feel so nervous about it, but I do. Last night, I caught myself starting to think that going to a dance was almost as bad as getting up in front of the class to make a presentation. It isn't. But I spent last night tossing and turning and then tossing and turning some more, anyway.

The dance is the only thing the girls in my class have talked about for days—choosing new outfits, styling hair, learning how to dance. Yikes! Oh, and then Addison and Madison keep dropping loud hints about how they can't wait for everyone, especially me, to see what the theme is. It's obvious that it's a secret. And by the way they're acting, it's also obvious that it's not going to be good.

"So I made a baseball card of myself," Sam says. "There's a picture of me in my uniform on the front and all of my information on the back like my stats from this season, my height and weight, and my hometown. I also have my team on here—Team Bradshaw—my mom, my dad, and my sister Lily." Sam shuffles from foot to foot for a minute. Then he looks up and grins. I guess that means he's done.

"Okay. Good job, Sam," says Mr. Summer. "I like how you made your portrait about doing something you enjoy. Does anyone have questions or comments for Sam?"

If I open my mouth, I might blurt something about how cute Sam looks today. So I keep quiet. Addison doesn't.

"Sam, your presentation was amazing. And that's such a good picture of you; you look really cute in that uniform," she says and giggles.

All the girls giggle.

Sam's smile fades as he bites his lip and looks down at the ground. The tips of his ears are red. I remember that he wanted his presentation to be taken seriously. I don't think it was.

"Well, if that's all for Sam, let's hear from Taylor next. Taylor, you're up," says Mr. Summer.

Taylor walks to the front of the room and sets up her presentation. She looks different today. We all do. Everyone's wearing what they'll wear to the dance. To me, we all look like it's picture day.

Looking at Taylor today makes me feel like I'm looking at Taylor in the future. She looks older somehow, and prettier. She's wearing a red and orange striped skirt that only Taylor could wear. And her hair is pulled back into a low ponytail with a couple of stray curls popping out around her face. She's even wearing lip-gloss. It all makes her look kind of unfamiliar. Then, she smiles and there's my best friend again.

Taylor unveils her presentation. She takes everyone through the pictures and photos and talks about how they represent her. So far, it's like she showed me before we went shopping. Then she pauses for a long time. When she starts talking again, something about her voice is different. Softer. And her smile—it's her Zach smile.

"Right now, the most important role in my life is being a big sister. Most of you know I have a little brother, Zach. He's four. But only one of you really knows Zach. My brother has autism. This means he has a lot of trouble with people and feel-ings and communication. It means that he has challenges that I don't have, that none of us have. And for a while, I didn't want anyone to know," says Taylor. She stops and blinks a few times.

"I didn't want anyone to know," she says again. "But now what I want all of you to know is Zach is smart and funny and sweet. He knows more about dinosaurs than anyone I know and he's my favorite person to make ice cream sundaes with. I'm proud of Zach. And I'm proud to be his big sister." This time her smile is big and bright, and not at all sad.

When Taylor finishes, Mr. Summer clears his throat. Twice. He says, "That was wonderful, Taylor. Zach is lucky to have you for his big sister." Mr. Summer's voice sounds funny, kind of like he has a cold.

When Taylor sits down behind me, I turn around and say, "I didn't know you were going to do that. It was perfect."

She grins at me and says one word, "Cannonball." It's a challenge.

Jenna is next. She wants to be an astronaut so it's perfect that her self-portrait is a picture of her face on the planet Mars. She'll get there.

"Okay class, our last presentation for today will be Lacey's. The floor is yours," says Mr. Summer.

An easel stands in the corner turned toward the wall. Lacey walks over and turns it around. It's a painting of two girls—a good painting. I'd almost forgotten Lacey is an artist.

Lacey says, "This is my self-portrait. It's two different pictures of me. This one is me in my old life in Ohio." It's the picture on the left. That picture shows Lacey looking like she did when she first moved here with longer wavy hair. The thing I notice first though is how big the smile is on that Lacey. "This one on the right is me now. Here. In Michigan," she says. It's obvious in the picture and in her voice that she's still not happy here. That picture shows a girl who's not smiling at all. It's sad, and a little bit creepy, the way the two girls are looking at each other, one happy and one not.

After the presentations are over, Mr. Summer gives us a little extra time to get ready for the dance. Taylor, Jenna, Abby and I watch to see which bathroom Madison is going to use and then head for one at the other end of the hall.

We all line up in front of the mirror. Abby unbraids and rebraids her hair. Taylor slicks on another coat of lip-gloss. I look in the mirror and try to decide if I like what I see. After a lot of trying on, I found a dress I liked that also got yes votes from my mom and Taylor. It's a tank style dress made of a really comfortable stretchy material that my mom said is called jersey. It's the softest sky blue and it's short enough but not too short. But the best part of my outfit is my shoes. My mom found a pair of ballet flats that are the same pale blue with white polka dots—I love them. A little lip-gloss and one of Daisy's less-fancy barrettes in my hair for some sparkle and I'm as good as I'm going to get.

I see Taylor watching me in the mirror. As usual, she reads my mind. "You look really pretty," she says. "Don't worry about anything. We'll have fun."

"Taylor's right. You look great," says Jenna. "Now are we ready to go find out what the secret theme is? I don't think I could stand to listen to them whisper and snicker about it for one more day."

"I guess," I say. "I have a bad feeling about it, though."

"I'm sure it's fine," says Abby. Her words are confident, but the way she says them sounds like she's trying to convince herself, too.

So we head toward the cafeteria where the dance is. My first dance. I can already feel my palms start to sweat. That's going to be gross if anyone actually does ask me to dance.

When we get to the cafeteria, Mr. Summer stands in front of the still-closed doors. His arms are crossed tightly across his chest and tufts of his hair stick up like he's been tugging on it. Mrs. Marinelli, Mrs. Kim, and my mom stand off to the side. Nobody's smiling. My mom looks like she's trying not to cry.

"There's not going to be a dance this afternoon." Mr. Summer's voice is loud enough to be heard above all the chatter.

We all go silent for two beats and then everyone starts talking at once. "What?" "Why?" "No dance?"

Taylor leans close and hisses, "Something's up."

I nod.

Mr. Summer raises his hands and waits for everyone to stop talking.

"No dance. I'm not going to explain why other than to say that I am extremely disappointed in two of your classmates and very proud of another."

Mrs. Marinelli suddenly stomps off down the hall. And after a longish pause, Mrs. Kim follows her. My mom stays put.

It's only then that I notice two things. The first is that Madison and Addison aren't here. And the second is that Lacey is standing right next to Mr. Summer, separate from the rest of the class.

"We're going to go back to the classroom now."
Everyone groans. "Don't worry, I'm not going to
make you do work. We'll raid the games cup-
boards and, if Mrs. Humphrey will help me, we'll
still serve the refreshments."

My mom smiles, wipes her eyes, and smiles
bigger this time.

The rest of the afternoon was kind of weird,
but fun. After she helped Mr. Summer schlep the
cupcakes, bags of popcorn, and giant bowl full of
pink, fizzy punch from the cafeteria to our classroom, my mom left. Everyone fell on the food
like they hadn't eaten in days. Everyone, but
Lacey. She sat at her desk and read a book all
afternoon. I don't think she was actually reading,
though, because I never saw her turn a page.

Once we were full of sugar and carbonation,
we played Charades and even had an impromptu
spelling bee using only words that started with
the letter "p." I won—the word was *pneumonia*.

It wasn't until the end of the day, when we
were packing up to go home and still laughing
about Sam slipping and sliding across the room
after stepping in frosting that I noticed: Madison
and Addison never came back to class.

"Mom?" I hang my backpack on the hook, and point feet toward the kitchen. "Mom!" I know I'm bellowing, and I know my mom doesn't like bellowing, but I have questions for her—lots of questions.

"In here." My mom's voice is coming from the direction of the kitchen, but it sounds muffled, like she's inside a cupboard or something. I start talking while I make my way into and around the kitchen.

"Hey, Mom? What happened today? What did Madison and Addison do? And why did you look so mad? Mr. Summer wouldn't tell us anything. Not one thing. And when Jalen kept asking and asking why the dance got cancelled, Mr. Summer pretended he couldn't hear him. It was kind of funny. But really, what happened?"

"Mom?" I still don't see her. But now I hear shuffling and banging and muttering from around the corner in the laundry room.

"Mom? What are you doing?"

"Will you help me?" My mom is crouched next to the washing machine, lacing up her sneakers. She looks up at me, chewing on her lip just like Daisy does when she's nervous. My bike helmet is perched on her head and she's wearing knee pads, elbow pads and wrist guards.

"Help you what?" With that much padding and protection, I can't imagine what my mom's going to do.

"Ride my bike."

"Seriously?"

"Yep. I dusted it off—more than once. And I took it up to the bike shop for a tune up. It needed new tubes in the tires and they did something with the gears. But it's ready to go." She smiles one of those smiles that mean she's trying to talk me into something. "And so am I."

She's still sitting on the laundry room floor. Not looking anything like "ready to go." Maybe it's all the gear. But I reach out a hand and help her up. She squeezes my hand—hard—before she lets go.

"Hey, Mom?"

"Yes, honey?"

"Before we go outside, can I ask you something?"

"Of course."

"What happened at school?" I chew on my lip. "*Why* was the dance cancelled?"

"Oh, honey, were you disappointed?"

I think for a minute. "No, not exactly. It was just all so weird. And even though Mr. Summer didn't say anything, I kind of felt like it was my fault."

"Your fault? Why on earth would it be *your* fault?" My mom tucks my hair back behind my ears.

"Well, maybe not my fault exactly. But like it had something to do with me, especially after I saw how you were acting."

"It was Madison and Addison. They planned something . . . unkind." My mom's lips press together hard for a minute, then relax back into a smile. "It doesn't matter what. All that matters is that Lacey stopped it."

"Lacey?"

"Yes. Lacey went to Mr. Summer and told him what they had planned. She did the right thing."

"Lacey?"

"Lacey. She was very brave." One more tucking of my hair behind my ear and my mom reaches for the back door. "Forgiving can be hard to do. But if you do—when you do—something tells me Lacey is going to prove to be a good friend for a long time."

"Lacey?" I can't stop saying it. I'm just so surprised. Even though Lacey apologized and I guess tried to explain, I didn't think she really meant it.

"Now how about that bike riding lesson?"

I laugh and follow my mom out the door. "Let's go!"

word #1000

authentic

real, genuine, or true

I smell pancakes. My mom makes pancakes for breakfast on the first day and the last day of school every year. I love my mom's pancakes. They're light and fluffy and she warms up the syrup. Yum. I put on my uniform for the last time as a fifth grader, brush my hair and head downstairs to get my share of the pancakes before Daisy eats them all.

I walk in the kitchen and see Daisy shoveling pancakes into her mouth as fast as she can.

"Oink, Daisy. Mom, are there any left for me?"

"Sit down and drink your juice," says my mom. She waves her spatula in the air, showing off the three princess band-aids on her arm from her one big fall yesterday. "I've got a stack coming just for you. And Daisy, please chew with your mouth closed."

I do as I'm told and sit down in the seat that has been mine since I graduated from my high-chair a million years ago. Next to my placemat is something that looks like a present. It's a blue box with a wide yellow ribbon tied around it. "What's this?" I ask.

"Mom got us last day of school presents," says Daisy. "Mine is this charm bracelet. See? It has a ballerina charm and a daisy flower charm. And mom said I can get more charms to add to it. Isn't it great?"

It is. It's just the kind of thing Daisy loves.

"It's really pretty," I say. "Mom? Last day of school presents? That's new."

"I decided to start a new tradition. You girls have had great years and Dad and I are proud of you. So I thought it would be fun to get each of you a little present. Open yours already."

My mom is not a patient present opener. She's a ripper. I savor gifts. I take longer than anyone to work through my pile on Christmas morning. It drives my mom crazy.

"Okay, here goes." I untie the ribbon and lay it aside. Then I open the box. Inside is what looks like a book. It has a pale blue leather cover with my initials stamped on it in shiny gold. It's the

size of one of my school notebooks. And it's filled
with blank pages.

"Thanks, Mom," I say. "It's really pretty. I love
the color. Is it a journal?" I've always kind of
thought about keeping a journal, but never figured out what to write about.

"You're about to reach one thousand words in
your collection, right?"

I nod, not quite sure how my mom knew, but
happy that she did.

"Well, this is a special notebook for you to collect your next thousand."

Wow. My mom understands how important
my collection is to me. And now I have someplace
special to collect even more words. Wow. "Thanks
Mom. Really, thanks. I love it," I say.

"Good. Now eat your pancakes," she says and
gives me a quick kiss on the top of my head.

I look at the one thousandth word in my notebook and sigh. I wish I had picked another day to
do my presentation because if I had picked
another day, it would already be over. But, I didn't.
I picked today.

Taylor arrives with the morning bell. Good—no
time to talk. I know she wants to ask me about
my presentation and I don't want to talk about it.

I decided for sure, well almost for sure, to give my safe presentation. It's what I practiced last night. It's me as the main character in a book. I think I'll get a good grade. But it's not the presentation Taylor wants me to give—the "go for it" version, the "real me" version. She's going to say I chickened out. That's why I don't want to talk about it. That's why I smile at her as she scrambles to her seat and then pretend to look for something in my desk.

"Well Taylor, thank you for keeping things exciting right up until the end," says Mr. Summer. He smiles and shuts the door.

"Today we'll hear from our last three presenters," says Mr. Summer. "And then we'll say farewell to this year's Fifth Farewell." He chuckles at his joke. No one else does.

"Okay," says Mr. Summer. "Madison, Oliver, and Annie are presenting today. Do the three of you want to decide who goes first?"

"I'm first," says Madison without looking at Oliver or me. "I want to go first."

"Okay. Madison's first. How about Oliver and then Annie to wind things up?" asks Mr. Summer.

So, I'm going last. Great, more time to think about it.

Madison sashays to the front of the room like she's on a fashion runway. She flicks a button and the TV screen fills with her face—picture after picture of her in different poses and outfits. A sameness about the pictures makes me think they were all taken on the same day. After a few minutes, it's over. Madison smirks. She hasn't said anything.

Mr. Summer clears his throat. "Well, Madison. That was interesting. Can you tell us why that video was your self-portrait?"

"I told you there was no way one picture could capture me. So I made a video of a bunch of different shots of me. Don't you get it?" she asks.

Uh, no. I don't think anyone gets it. And really, I don't think there's anything to get.

Mr. Summer scratches his head, adjusts his glasses, and looks at the ceiling. Then he sighs. His sigh sounds like how I imagine disappointment sounds. "Okay Madison, thank you. You can take your seat." And she does. Addison tells her how great her video was. It sounds like she even believes it.

"And now, Oliver. You're up," says Mr. Summer.

Oliver. I forget to be nervous about my presentation because I want to hear what he has to say.

"My two older sisters dragged me to the mall last weekend," Oliver says, "and while they tried on every pair of shoes they could find, I wandered around. Next to the hot pretzel stand, there was an artist doing drawings of people. So I asked him to do one of me."

Oliver holds a canvas in front of him, but the back of the picture faces us. Now, he turns it around. Everyone laughs.

"It's a caricature," says Oliver. "A caricature takes something about the person being drawn and exaggerates it so that it's the only thing you see. For me, he picked my dimple."

The drawing looks enough like Oliver that you know it's him—the cowlick in the front of his hair, the brown eyes that crinkle when he smiles, and, yes, the dimple. It looks like a deep hole, a crater, in his cheek. It makes his face look lopsided, like the two sides don't belong to the same person.

"I think sometimes people see each other like caricatures. We take one thing about a person and make it the biggest thing, the only thing that matters. For example, some people think of Sam as only being funny or Jenna as only being smart or Taylor as only being loud," he says.

Taylor laughs at that one. Loudly.

"And me," says Oliver. "I'm nice. That's all I ever hear about myself. Oliver is nice. And I am nice. But there's more to me than nice. Just like there's more to Sam, Jenna, and Taylor than being funny or smart or loud."

I can't stop looking at Oliver. He's right. He's a lot more than just nice.

"I present to you my anti self-portrait. One thing about a person is never the whole story," says Oliver. He puts the caricature facedown on Mr. Summer's desk.

After a few beats of silence, most of us start clapping. Mr. Summer says, "Oliver, that was outstanding. You showed a true understanding of the project and went at it your own way. Well done."

Oliver shoves his hands in his pockets and struggles to hide a huge smile. And that dimple—it's deeper than ever. And that's a good thing.

"Annie, are you ready?" Mr. Summer asks.

Am I ready? No, not really. But there's no way to put it off any longer. It's time. I start to stand up, then sit back down in my desk long enough to slip my book report-style project back into my desk and pull something else out.

I walk up to the front of the room and perch on the edge of Mr. Summer's desk, holding my battered notebook in front of me like a shield. I try to act casual but the truth is I'm not sure if my legs will support me—they're shaking. And when I start talking, my voice shakes, too. But I keep going anyway.

"For me, words are stronger than pictures. Words are more beautiful than pictures. They're powerful. Words can make you hear, smell, taste, and feel. And words can definitely make you see," I say.

I see some confused looks and some bored looks, but enough interested faces to keep going.

"Okay, how about this? Like if I tell you I was sitting outside one morning when a breeze shook the leaves in the tree just enough to make them rustle, can you hear it?"

I look at Mr. Summer. He nods and smiles.

"Or, if I tell you that when I hug my grandma, she smells like apple crisp and lavender soap, can you smell her?"

Now I get more nods including one with a smile from Oliver.

"Using the right word to describe something makes a difference. Like, right now I'm nervous. But the word nervous doesn't tell you exactly how I feel. If I tell you that when I first came up here I was petrified but now I've settled down to just jittery, that tells you more," I say. And laugh a little. A few kids laugh too.

"Words, the right words, can make pictures. I tried to explain this to Sam last week and we ended up talking about baseball. I used words to describe certain parts of a game I saw so that he felt like he was part of it. He could see my picture in his mind," I say.

"It was awesome. The slide into third was the best," says Sam.

"You're probably thinking this has nothing to do with a self-portrait. But you're wrong. I don't agree with the saying 'a picture is worth a thousand words.'" I open my notebook and fan through the pages. "I've collected one thousand words and, when I looked at them, really looked at them, I saw that my words *are* me. And they make more than just one picture of me."

I stand up straight, take a deep breath, and in that moment I know exactly what I'm going to say. It's not what I practiced or what I thought I was going to say. And it sure doesn't feel safe. Still, I jump.

"*Authentic*. That's the word I collected this morning. My one thousandth word. Authentic is what I am and more than anything else, it's what my word pictures say about me. Being authentic means being who you really are. It means that it's okay if someone thinks I'm a nerd, or boring, or just doesn't like me. It's okay because *I* like me."

Addison snickers.

I take another deep breath and keep going. "I know that I'm not a nerd or boring. And if someone doesn't want to be my friend, that doesn't mean there's anything wrong with me." I look right at Addison and Madison. Well, it looks like I'm going for it.

"There are words I collected because I liked the way they sounded or how they let me describe something exactly right. I collected funny words because I love to laugh, and words that reminded me of someone or something special because I treasure the important people and things in my life. I also have words that helped me when something hard happened. I want to be a writer and use my words to make pictures for other people," I say. All of this comes out in a rush. I'm out of breath and I don't know what to say next, since I wasn't planning to say any of that.

I look around the room. It's mostly what I expect to see: Taylor clapping and whooping, Mr. Summer smiling like he's proud of me, Addison and Madison whispering and snickering to each other, Oliver looking at me in a way that makes my heart beat even faster, Sam grinning. And then I see something I don't expect to see—Lacey, looking right at me and clapping. I can't read the look on her face. It's not quite a smile, but it's close. I smile back.

I jumped. I almost can't believe I did it. But I did. And it feels good. Better than good. As I walk back to my seat, I know what the first word in my new notebook will be—*exhilaration*.

The bell rings. And suddenly, fifth grade is over. Most of the kids rush toward the classroom door, whooping and giving Mr. Summer high fives on the way out. Behind me, Taylor hasn't moved.

"You did it." Her voice sounds surprised.

"Cannonball?" I ask. I try to stop my face from smiling. It doesn't work.

"Definitely." Taylor beams right back and then hops up from her seat. "Ready?"

"Almost."

I walk over to where Lacey sits tracing circles on her desk with her finger.

"So, Taylor and I have a kind of tradition."

"Yeah?"

I reach back and grab Taylor's wrist, half-dragging her over to stand next to me.

"Yeah. Every year, on the last day of school, we run all the way to my house, lie flat on our backs in the backyard, and do absolutely nothing," I say.

Lacey finally stands up.

"So your tradition is to do nothing?" She smiles, just a little bit.

"Not just nothing," says Taylor. "*Absolutely* nothing." She giggles. "Well, until we get hungry."

"Then we raid the fridge and spend the rest of the day making a list of all the awesome things we're going to do over the summer."

"Sounds pretty fun," says Lacey. She twirls a hunk of her hair which is back to being wavy, and there's no sign of a headband.

"So, are you coming?" I ask.

"Absolutely."

The three of us—my always best friend and my new-all-over-again friend swoop out the door.

Together.

Discussion Questions

1. Annie is a *logophile* (LOG-ah-file), a lover of words. Do you have a favorite word? Why is it your favorite?

2. What do you think Annie learned about herself? Her family members? Her friends?

3. Everyone is afraid of something: Annie is terrified to stand up in front of the class and talk. What are you afraid of? What do you do to deal with being nervous?

4. It can be hard to fit in *and* be yourself. How did the decisions Lacey and Madison make express who they were? How did their choices affect how others saw them? Do you think different choices would have led to different results?

5. Madison and Addison seem to enjoy being mean to Annie. Have you ever encountered someone who behaves the way they do? Do you think there may be reasons why someone might choose to act that way?

6. Annie and Taylor have been best friends for some time and Lacey just moved into town. What does being a true friend mean to you?

How do you make a friend? How do you keep a friend?

7. Annie is convinced she will never be able to live down the embarrassing incident that happened to her in the second grade. Is she right? What does it take for you to allow yourself—or someone else—to move on?

8. There were many instances of characters wanting to keep something secret—Taylor not wanting anyone to know about Zach's autism; Madison not wanting anyone to know she needs extra help with schoolwork; Lacey not wanting Annie and Taylor to know her parents are getting a divorce. How did "not telling" affect the character herself? How did it affect the other characters in the story?

9. Annie thinks that Taylor is bold and sure of herself because she's loud and outspoken. Do you agree with Annie? Who else in the story showed courage? When and how? What helps you when you don't feel brave?

10. If you were a student in Annie's class and you had to complete the Fifth Farewell, what would you choose for a self-portrait? Why? What would you want others to know about you? Is there anything you wouldn't want to share?

Word Collection

#983 conundrum—[kuh-NUN-drum] a puzzling question or problem

I have to do a self-portrait, but I can't draw. That's just one of my conundrums.

#984 inkling—[INK-ling] a partial idea or understanding

I don't have my project all figured out, but I have an inkling of where to begin.

#985 discombobulated—[dis-kum-BAH-bue-lated] confused or disconcerted

Trying to think about too many things at once leaves my brain discombobulated.

#986 effervescent—[eh-fer-VES-sint] bubbling, lively and sparkling

When I stand next to my effervescent little sister, I look even more boring than I actually am.

#987 juxtapose—[JUHK-stah-pose] to put side by side for comparison or contrast

If you juxtapose my room with Lacey's, you can tell which one of us has lived here our whole lives.

#988 trepidation—[treh-puh-DAY-shun] a condition of anxiety or dread; alarm

Just hearing someone talk about the Fifth Farewell project fills me with trepidation.

#989 shindig—[SHIN-dig] a party or dance

The shindig we gave for Taylor's birthday meant a lot to her.

#990 blindsided—[BLIND-sie-ded] attacked where a person is vulnerable

I never expected to be blindsided by someone I thought could be a new friend.

#991 flabbergasted—[FLA-ber-gas-ted]
overcome with surprise and bewilderment

The conversation my mom had with Mrs.
Marinelli left me flabbergasted.

#992 steadfast—[STED-fast] able to be trusted or
relied on; loyal

Real friends like Taylor are steadfast and loyal.

#993 ambush—[AM-bush] a sudden and unexpected attack from a concealed position

This whole school dance thing feels a lot like an
ambush.

#994 haven—[HAY-ven] a place of safety,
shelter, or comfort

Sometimes I just need to find a haven where I
can think things through.

#995 neophyte—[NEE-uh-fite] a beginner or
novice at any activity

When it comes to knowing who to trust, I guess
I'm still a neophyte.

#996 mettle—[MEH-tl] boldness, strength of character

I don't have the mettle to stand up to people who make me miserable.

#997 audacious—[aw-DAY-shus] very bold or adventurous; daring

If I were audacious, getting up in front of the class would be a piece of cake.

#998 perspective—[per-SPEK-tiv] the way things are seen from a particular point of view

Am I wrong, or is my perspective really different from just about everyone else's?

#999 illuminate—[ih-LOO-meh-nate] to make clear or easier to understand; explain

The right word illuminates whatever I'm trying to say.

#1000 authentic—[aw-THEN-tic] real, genuine or true

Mom says you have to face your fears to be your authentic self.

#1001 . . .

Marilee Haynes lives with her husband and three young children just outside Charlotte, North Carolina. *Pictures of Me* is her third novel for young people. Her critically acclaimed first title, *a.k.a. Genius*, was published by Pauline Teen in 2013, followed by the popular sequel *Genius under Construction* in 2014. A full-time, stay-at-home mom, she writes during stolen, quiet moments (in other words, when everyone else is asleep).

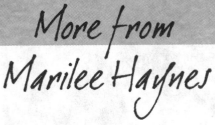

More from
Marilee Haynes

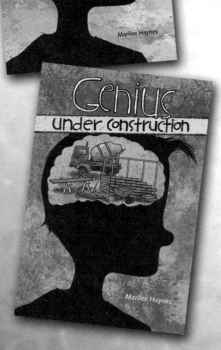

"*A.K.A. Genius* is a good book because it deals with situations that kids like me go through every day. There are so many situations that are funny, embarrassing, stressful, happy, sad, and exciting in this book … just like real life."

— Charlie B., 10,
attends Catholic school
in North Carolina

"Gabe could be the kid sitting next to me in any one of my classes or I could see myself in his shoes as parts of the story unfold."

— Sean L., 13,
attends a public middle
school in Michigan

Who are the Daughters of St. Paul?

We are Catholic sisters with a mission. Our task is to bring the love of Jesus to everyone like Saint Paul did. You can find us in over 50 countries. Our founder, Blessed James Alberione, showed us how to reach out to the world through the media. That's why we publish books, make movies and apps, record music, broadcast on radio, perform concerts, help people at our bookstores, visit parishes, host JClub book fairs, use social media and the Internet, and pray for all of you.

Visit our Web site at www.pauline.org

BOOKS & MEDIA

The Daughters of St. Paul operate book and media centers at the following addresses. Visit, call, or write the one nearest you today, or find us at www.pauline.org.

CALIFORNIA
3908 Sepulveda Blvd, Culver City, CA 90230   310-397-8676
935 Brewster Avenue, Redwood City, CA 94063   650-369-4230
5945 Balboa Avenue, San Diego, CA 92111   858-565-9181

FLORIDA
145 SW 107th Avenue, Miami, FL 33174   305-559-6715

HAWAII
1143 Bishop Street, Honolulu, HI 96813   808-521-2731

ILLINOIS
172 North Michigan Avenue, Chicago, IL 60601   312-346-4228

LOUISIANA
4403 Veterans Memorial Blvd, Metairie, LA 70006   504-887-7631

MASSACHUSETTS
885 Providence Hwy, Dedham, MA 02026   781-326-5385

MISSOURI
9804 Watson Road, St. Louis, MO 63126   314-965-3512

NEW YORK
64 West 38th Street, New York, NY 10018   212-754-1110

SOUTH CAROLINA
243 King Street, Charleston, SC 29401   843-577-0175

TEXAS
Currently no book center; for parish exhibits or outreach evangelization, contact: 210-569-0500 or SanAntonio@paulinemedia.com or P.O. Box 761416, San Antonio, TX 78245

VIRGINIA
1025 King Street, Alexandria, VA 22314   703-549-3806

CANADA
3022 Dufferin Street, Toronto, ON M6B 3T5   416-781-9131

Smile
God loves you!